Madrona

Dear Reader,

When I read and evaluate manuscripts, I am considering a myriad of storytelling traits: the cadence of sentences, the narrator's acuity, the accumulation of plot points, and so on. But usually, I'm simply hoping to be won over. Irrespective of genre, structure, or length, the stories that engender a sense of trust—that assure me I'm in capable hands—are so often my favorites.

Kevin Allardice's *Weft* has won me over in this way. Which is a funny thing to say: a novel about a con woman has made me trust it more deeply than nearly any other book I can recall reading. But as you'll discover, there's more to Bridget than the con she and her son carry out in malls across America.

Weft is many things. It's a mother-son novel. It's a Halloween thriller. It's a dose of 90s nostalgia replete with malls, Star Wars references, and Kinko's. And it's a story about belonging. *How far will we go to avoid rejection? To whom do we align ourselves? What do we think exists beyond the horizon of "one more lie"?* That's the incredible thing about Allardice's book: It can make you laugh, gasp, and murmur in assent all in the span of one scene.

I hope you enjoy this novel as much as I have. Whether you are a bookseller, reviewer, librarian, or neighborhood book-club organizer, please feel free to reach out to me. I mean that sincerely—this is Madrona Books' inaugural publication, and I'd love nothing more than to discuss *Weft* with other enthusiasts.

Kevin Breen

Kevin Breen
Publisher, Madrona Books
kevin@madronabooks.com

A note to reviewers: Please remember that these proofs are uncorrected and that changes may be made before the book is printed. If any material from the book is to be quoted in a review, please check it against the text in the final bound book, which will be sent to you when it is ready. For media inquiries, speaking engagements, and book club queries,
please contact Kevin Breen: kevin@madronabooks.com

WEFT

Also by Kevin Allardice

The Ghosts of Bohemian Grove
Any Resemblance to Actual Persons
Family, Genus, Species
As the Ceiling Flew Away

REC●

A NOVEL

WEFT

PM 07:49
OCT. 31 97

Kevin
Allardice

Weft

This is a work of fiction. Names, places, locations, and incidents are products of the author's imagination or are used fictitiously. As such, this novel is not to be construed as real. Any resemblance to actual events, places, people, or organizations is entirely coincidental.

For permissions contact: editor@madronabooks.com

Book and cover design by Kevin Breen

ISBN: 978-1-960593-00-9
Cataloging-in-Publication Data is available upon request

Manufactured in the United States of America

Published by
Madrona Books, Olympia, Washington
www.madronabooks.com

1.

Looking for the right look meant looking for what could not be seen; the intangibles were the tell.

"I still don't know what that means," Jake said.

Bridget stacked the dozen or so index cards; each was paperclipped to a Polaroid. They'd gotten sticky from the spilled soda. At least she hoped it was soda. In this food court—which was overlit as if in a futile attempt to sterilize the place—all surfaces felt tacky as flypaper.

"These," she said, pointing to a Polaroid, "aren't for us. They're for them." She nodded her chin at the denizens of the Foothill Square Mall, those waiting in line at the Panda Express, those waiting in line at the Sbarro Pizza, and those whose indecision seemed not just culinary but existential: Whether today was a Panda Express day or a Sbarro Pizza day, who knew? "It makes it real for them. They get to see another possibility for themselves. An idea of themselves to try on for size."

Around them, the younger mall-goers were excitedly holding the costumes they'd bought from the Spirit Halloween Outlet. It was clear that most of the costumes were the usual fare, easily accommodating basic categories: the random artifacts of domestic ephemera turned, lunatically, into something wearable. (Here was a kid carrying a ketchup bottle costume.) Then there were the kids gripping cheap, mass-produced masks of characters from recent animated movies, characters whose unrecognizability seemed proof enough of their timeliness. Those uncanny faces were the closest gestures, if unintentional, to the kind of horror that Bridget believed to be the true meaning of the holiday. They reminded her of the Halloween parties of her youth. Indeed, she lamented the increasing turning away from horror that she was witnessing here, lamenting it with the fervor of an a.m.-radio evangelical railing against the secularization of Christmas. That kind of horror—so pure you only really encountered it in childhood—was not just about zombies somnambulating hungrily toward you or a chainsaw-wielding maniac in a mask collaged from the flesh of his victims. It was also about the abjection of the body.

She turned her attention back to Jake, the table between them.

She idly sifted through the Polaroids and index cards. Each picture was of someone from the shoulders up trying to look their best, captured in the worst possible film stock, in the worst possible light. Casting directors using Polaroids seemed almost cruel, but it was standard industry practice.

"We're looking—you're looking—for something that can't be found here." She held up one photo of a kid who appeared to have only learned how to smile yesterday and was still not entirely confident in the basic muscle mechanics of it. "Sean here," Bridget said, reading the info that Sean had written on the index card paperclipped to his photo, "might be perfect, but there's no way of telling from this."

The index card had Sean's full name (Sean Johansson), age (fifteen), height (five-eight, the eight appearing to have been furiously written over a seven), and his phone number (no area code provided).

Jake tended to his Mountain Dew, sucking it up as if trying to pull the entire world through the straw. By the time he set it down, he was a little out of breath. "Can't you just tell me what I'm looking for?"

Bridget waved a dismissive hand at the rest of the food court. "You can't be so literal-minded."

"Yes, I can."

She flipped to the next Polaroid and contact card. Another boy, maybe Jake's age, maybe younger, excitedly stared into the camera like he was going to eat it. She flipped to the next one, then set the stack down.

"Okay," Bridget said. "You remember Lion?"

Jake tore the plastic cap from his cup and tipped ice into his mouth, crunched it.

Bridget said, "Remember when we took Lion out to that dog park? The one in Aurora?"

"The nice one."

"How he just barreled into other dogs, tripped over his own legs?"

"So what."

"So? So you're sitting on a French fry."

"No, I'm not."

"Look."

Jake obeyed. He stood up just enough to see a smushed fry—three or four, really—on his seat. He brushed the seat of his pants, swept the fries to the floor.

"So that's most people," Bridget said. "Lion tumbling through the world, no clue where his body stopped and the rest of the world started."

Jake sat back down, crunched more ice, open-mouthed.

"Now," Bridget said. "Remember that husky? You said—do you remember this?—he looked like a stuffy. That dog was so beautiful you thought it was a toy."

"It had different colored eyes."

"Remember the way it moved. Effortless. It understood the relationship between its body and the world around it, had been taught from a young age, to the extent that the world seemed to distort itself around that dog."

"I remember you said David Bowie also had different colored eyes."

Bridget smacked the Polaroids, felt the pinch of a staple beneath her palm. "What's your point, Jake?"

"I thought *you* were making a point." Jake tried to tip some more ice into his mouth, but the cup was clearly empty.

"You're looking for a purebred," Bridget said, grabbing the cup from him.

Jake hunched, folded his arms on the sticky table. "I miss Lion."

"You never walked him."

"Can I get a refill?"

"Get a water."

"That husky—you said he'd die soon, anyway."

"What?"

"You said purebreds are designed to look nice and die. You said only mutts like Lion survive."

"Well, it's true."

"But Lion died." Jake grabbed the cup and stood up. "I'm gonna get a refill."

"Get water."

"I'm thirsty for soda."

"Because you don't drink water."

Jake walked away. He'd been developing an odd lope in his gait, as if one foot had fallen asleep. This had become such a habit that his left Chuck Taylor was wearing down faster than his right. It seemed like an affectation, not so much that he couldn't bear to lift each foot off the ground when walking, but that he couldn't bear to be seen as someone who'd care enough to lift each foot off the ground when walking. Or at least she hoped it was an affectation; if it wasn't, it might be some sort of neurological or muscular disorder emerging. She quickly cataloged her family history and Tod's family history for unnaturally bent postures, gaits gone awry. The postures of their progenitors were ramrod-straight. Jake wandered toward the counter of Hot Dog on a Stick, ignoring the line.

He'd gotten his soda there, when he could have gotten it anywhere, because he admitted he liked the way the girls behind the counter looked in those uniforms. It had been a strange moment, an admission perhaps accidentally offered, but one that Jake chose to own, embrace. "They look good," Bridget had said, and Jake had nodded. She now remained at their table, watching Jake hand his creased cup over to the girl (his age, she imagined) who was too bewildered by him to ask him to go to the end of the line and be patient like a normal person. Bridget was happy that he'd been able to admit to her something as simple as attraction. It occurred to her that if they'd never left Denver, if they were slogging through the stations of that life, he never would have admitted to something like the emergence of an erotic preference or aesthetic, be it that of gingham-uniformed Hot Dog on a Stick girls or another attraction. That was something.

He was walking back to her now, but at an oblique angle. He was angling to walk past her. When he approached, his eyes remained fixed on the mall beyond, and he said, "I'm gonna get a massage," passing in the direction of the Sharper Image.

"Rendezvous spot at one," she said.

"Yeah," he said, his voice dimmed by Doppler.

The rendezvous spot was always the fountain at the center of the mall, and no matter what town they were in, no matter what mall was festooned onto that town like a bow on a turd, there was always a fountain at the center of the mall. It always glittered with pennies and bottle caps.

Bridget gathered the Polaroids and contact cards into a large manila envelope and put it into her canvas tote bag. In there, she had blank contact cards, a Polaroid camera, and three packs of film, along with her wallet, keys, and a granola bar.

She left the food court, emerged from that aroma of grease and MSG, and headed down the wing of the mall where she was pretty sure they had the bookstore. She wanted to scan the movie magazines; if there was any news about the *Star Wars* prequels, she'd have to be abreast of it. And it also couldn't hurt to peruse the sci-fi section. The *Star Wars* spin-off novels were multiplying like gremlins, and last week a kid who smelled like tuna fish interrogated her about some niche corner of the universe that sounded like he was just putting random syllables together. Of course, her official response to all such questioning was that she wasn't permitted to divulge anything, but she was concerned that her incredulity at the names this kid was dropping betrayed her. Flipping through a few chapters of that mass-market pulp might help her not bark out a laugh when the next nerd began speaking in Tatooine-inspired tongues.

"Miss."

The bookstore was right up ahead, its entrance clotted with standees and magazine racks.

"Miss."

She was suddenly looking at a laminated photo, the size of a place mat, of a beach lined with palm trees—the blues so blue, the greens so green, the sand so beige.

"Miss, hello." The voice was chipper but insistent, and it was coming out of a mouth inches from her face. "How's this look, huh?" That mouth was embedded in a face that featured a patina of acne. He was walking backward to keep up with her. "You look like you could use a vacation. How would you like the opportunity for an all-expense paid trip to the lap of luxury? Of course you would."

She stopped. He stopped. The picture was still between them. She said, "Can I give you some advice?"

"Well, this vacation is closer than you imagine," he said, clearly just barreling through his script.

She grabbed the laminated picture from his hand. "Ditch that line, how I look like I could use a vacation."

"I'm sorry?" He—his name tag said *Ben*—was wearing baggy khakis and a maroon polo, tucked in. He tightened the tuck, as if just to do something with his hands.

"When you tell me that, that I look like I could use a vacation, you tell me I look tired. You tell me I look tired, I tell you to get lost. I walk away and I take your commission with me. Now—"

Ben was holding his chest as if anticipating a punch.

"Try that again." She handed the laminated picture back to him.

His exhalation was controlled, cautious.

"It's okay," she said. "You got this. Breathe. Start from the beginning, and just focus on what you want. So what do you want?"

"I—" He looked at the picture: the beach, the calming waves you could almost hear whispering in your ear. "I want you to sign up for a raffle. It's through Vespucci Travel. If you win, you can go here." He held up the picture, the wrong side facing Bridget.

"See?" she said. "That was so much better. Direct, simple, no weird judgments about my appearance."

"I'm really sorry about that."

"Again, you're focusing on the wrong thing. Focus on the next thing you want. Which is?"

He looked back to his kiosk: about the size of a golf cart, decorated with pictures of dream vacations that looked like screen savers. "Here." He grabbed a clipboard from the kiosk. A pen dangled on a thin ball-chain.

"Always keep it moving," Bridget said.

She took the clipboard and began filling out the form. After writing her complete name, she wrote her address as clearly as possible, her old Denver address. She didn't care about winning some unwinnable raffle; she just wanted to make sure mail with her name on it kept arriving there.

"So," Ben said over her shoulder, the scent of his Speed Stick as cloying as a prom date's boner. "Bridget from Denver. Love it there. What are you doing out here?"

She was imagining Tod pulling an envelope from the mailbox and—she was suddenly halfway through writing her social security number on this form, this form that was for a raffle, this form that was just a dumb promotion for a travel company, this form that was asking for increasingly personal details, this form that was a—

"Scam."

She apparently said that aloud, as Ben quickly said, "What?"

She pulled the paper from the clipboard and crumpled it into a ball.

"Don't you want a vacation?"

There was a binder on the kiosk, maybe full of all the

information of all the other suckers Ben had hooked today. She grabbed it.

"Miss!" Ben now had one hand on her wrist, the other on the binder. "Miss, what are—"

She pulled the binder out of his grip, but she lost control of it. Hitting the floor, it slid away—the tiled floors recently waxed perhaps—until it hit a pair of Chuck Taylors.

"Mom?"

Distracted by Jake's sudden entrance, Bridget took her eyes off the binder and Ben quickly snatched it up, shuffling back to the safety of his kiosk.

She said, "Jake!"

Jake said, "D'you sign us up for one of those vacations or something?"

She grabbed his arm and guided him swiftly away from the kiosk, toward a trash can against the wall. She unballed the form and began tearing it into tiny pieces, depositing just some of the confetti into the trash can, then—

"Follow me."

She guided him to the next trash can, this one between the Gap and Baby Gap, where she deposited another handful.

"I got one," Jake said.

She tried to relax a bit. She hadn't even written down her full social.

"I found someone I think would be good," Jake said. "He really has the look of Aniston."

"Anakin," Bridget said.

"Yeah." He pointed into the Gap. "Cargo shorts."

Jake must have been referring to the kid in cargo shorts browsing the cargo shorts table. He was about fifteen or sixteen (there really was no telling, of course, but he read as fifteen or sixteen), and he was moving with an aimlessness that wasn't weighed down by boredom; it was buoyed by something—something else. Jake was right. This kid did have the right look. Not that he looked like he could play Anakin Skywalker in the recently announced *Star Wars* prequels. She had no idea. She didn't even know what age the real casting directors would be searching for; no one did. No one knew anything about the films other than they'd have a young Anakin; all the rest was secret, which was exactly why this worked. But this kid did have the right look. It was the look of money. He bore the intangibles of confidence, of owning the space around him, including ownership of whatever people happened to occupy that space. It was a confidence that could only be bought.

"Excuse me," Bridget said ten minutes later, approaching him by the rack of flannels. "Hi. My name is Sarah."

She had the cargo shorts kid's attention now, though his studied look of indifference told her she only had it for the briefest of moments.

"This might sound like a crazy question, but have you done any acting?"

The sheer unexpectedness of this question bought her some more time. "What?"

"You're really quite striking, and—" She made a show of interrupting herself to explain: "I'm a casting director, so I'm just good at noticing people, people who maybe aren't in movies but maybe should be. You're definitely a *maybe should be.*"

He recoiled a bit, held on to the empty sleeve of a hanging flannel shirt as if to the hand of a parent. She might have come across a little too much like an old aunt drunkenly calling him handsome at Thanksgiving.

"This is going to sound crazy, but—do you know *Star Wars?*"

He shrugged. "My dad likes it."

"Well, they're doing what are called prequels, movies about all the stuff that happened before, and—you know Darth Vader?"

"Duh."

She had started to hunch closer to him. She righted her posture. "The project I'm working on now, I kinda have to be a little secretive about it. I'm not even allowed to show people the script. I mean, they didn't even give me the whole thing, just a couple scenes. But I can't even show those to someone unless they're doing a tape."

He let go of the flannel sleeve. "*Doing* a tape?"

"Auditioning. I record someone doing a reading of a scene, express ship the tape out to LucasFilm. Most people think George Lucas is in Hollywood, but he lives closer to San Francisco. D'you know that?"

"Reading a scene as Darth Vader, when he's like my age?"

"Before he got the mask, of course. Er, helmet."

She could see him imagining it, the portrait of an archvillain as a young man, starring Cargo Shorts Kid.

"And you wanna make a video of me doing it?"

Suddenly someone new was there, right there, beside him, angling her body between them. "Sorry, hello, hello." This was the boy's mother, had to be. "Can I help you? What's going on? Why are you talking to my son? Why did he just say you wanted to make a videotape of him?"

This woman—her chemically sweet perfume betraying their actual economic status—was moving menacingly closer to Bridget, who was slowly backing toward the store exit.

"I'm a casting director working on a very exciting new opportunity, and I was just chatting with, um, with—" She never got his name: first mistake, last mistake—"and um."

"Okay," the mom said, "I think you'd better just keep it moving. Okay, thanks!"

And just like that Bridget was out by the trash can between the Gap and the Baby Gap, a few hand-shredded bits of her old address still resting on the lip of the receptacle.

Jake walked up to her, sipping his soda.

"How many refills is that?" she said.

Jake looked over Bridget's shoulder, back into the store. "That didn't go right—not how it's supposed to work."

"Yes, Jake, I know that."

● **REC**

Pixels wash the frame clear. Bodies walk up a wall. Voices are made inaudible first by distance then by proximity, a voice now booming into a microphone, a sound that could consume the image. The frame moves, is reoriented. The bodies are no longer defying gravity, are now walking laterally across the frame, across a kitchen draped in blacks, oranges, reds.

2.

How it was supposed to work was the way it worked last time, over in Claymont.

That was at the harvest festival, held in the fairgrounds that had recently played host to some sort of rodeo and music festival. Between the harvest festival's booths selling hollowed gourd wind chimes, paper cups disintegrated in mounds of unidentifiable scat; Jake found a tooth.

The harvest festival might have seemed an odd choice to make a mark, as it boasted artifacts of a socioeconomic status unhelpful to Bridget's aims, but she'd brought Jake there because she knew the attendees would be more diverse than the domestic beer signs suggested. It was at the wine stomp where they found who they were looking for. Sitting bored on a bench, watching with his chin in his palm while adults stomped barefooted around a giant vat of Zinfandel grapes, the frothy result of their stomping sluicing from spigots into a series of large plastic tubs, was a kid, a teenage boy in jeans methodically torn. Whichever adult in this embarrassing display was his parent, this kid had surely heard his parents opine on the flintiness of a Sancerre.

This kid, Bridget would learn, was Ethan.

When she approached Ethan with her opening salvo—"Excuse me, hi. My name is Sarah. This might sound like a crazy question, but have you done any acting?"—he was more aloof than this kid in the Gap would be a week later. But after Bridget laced in the promises of *Star Wars*, and of being in front of the camera, and of there being some ineffable quality of his that no one had noticed before Bridget sat down next to him while bearing witness to a shameful display of parental drunkenness, he was warming up.

(This would work better on girls, Jake had said. "All that makeup. They're so vain." But he was wrong, and she hoped that Ethan here would help Jake understand how it was boys who were the best marks. If Ethan had a sister roughly the same age, she was surely already accustomed to strangers coming up to her in public, people remarking on her beauty, or speculating on her ambitions for a life in front of a camera. She might have even been someone who'd developed strategies for parrying away those advances, those comments, those invitations. On the other hand, boys had been trained in violence for so long, they were quietly aching to be told they were beautiful.)

Ethan said, "So do I have to memorize lines?"

"Just some," Bridget said. "It's a short scene we'd put you on tape for. And it's okay if you have the script in your hand. But of course, if they want to see you out in California—"

"Of course."

"Does memorizing make you nervous?"

"No! I was just asking. I know all the cheat codes to *Final Fantasy Six*—I memorize lots of shit."

She winced. It wasn't that she minded cursing. Indeed, it seemed to suggest a certain comfort the teen might feel with her that he didn't with other adults. But that was just it: She needed to cultivate a kind of chumminess with this kid that transcended the normal adult-teen dynamic, without abdicating the deference that dynamic typically conferred. And while she wanted to take comfort in the ease with which teen boys—her son included, now that she thought about it—cursed around her, she knew, like a substitute teacher, how easy it was to mistake complete disregard for evidence of camaraderie.

"Exactly," Bridget said. "No different than that."

"Kinda is, though," Ethan said. "Those are just codes."

"Words are just codes." Bridget shrugged.

That settled over Ethan like a cloud, a state of hypnosis broken only by his father sauntering over, holding his shoes, khakis rolled up above his squishy calf muscles, his bare feet stained maroon, breaded with dirt. He seemed to regard Bridget not as a threat but as a potential acquisition. "What'd you find here, Ethan?"

Ethan tried to explain Bridget's proposal, who she was and what she was offering, but the details were tripping over themselves, becoming reordered into a new causality.

"I'm a casting director," Bridget said, interrupting Ethan with a show of benevolence. "And I'd love to put Ethan on tape for a project I have."

"The new *Star Wars!*" Ethan said, his unabashed excitement aging him down a couple years.

His father, meanwhile, at the mention of this prospect, inflated his chest, actively fought back against his wine-drunk slouch. He promptly introduced himself as Bertram, not Bert, never Bert, and shook Bridget's hand with an aggressive jolt.

As she gave Bertram the dad's version of the pitch she'd given to Ethan—which was distinct from the mom's version—he began eyeing her in an unsettling way. Not the usual sideways leer she got from dads, but more like the way a makeup artist would assess the contours of your cheekbones, or a director of photography calibrating the penumbra on your nose from the backlight. Like you were a prop.

In the middle of her anecdote illustrating how George Lucas prefers actors who speak quickly, Bertram said, "I've seen you."

"Hm? Oh, I've been here all day," she said. "A girlfriend of mine from college does a crafts table here."

"*In a Pickle?*"

The words squeezed Bridget's heart as if it were a soggy sponge. "She mostly works with gourds and dried maize."

"The show, *In a Pickle*. When was that? Early eighties? Weren't you the daughter?"

Behind him, the last of the grape stompers were being helped out of the giant vat by very patient, railing-sturdy gentlemen.

"I'm not sure what you mean," she said.

"Sure!" Bertram had the confidence of a man who'd had an afternoon's worth of wine and a lifetime's worth of affirmation. "Aren't you her? I used to watch that show. You look good. Haven't really aged much. 'Cept around the neck a bit."

"Well," Bridget said, touching her throat, "thank you, but you must have me mistaken for someone else."

In her past life she'd figured out how to laugh people away from the topic of those two seasons of a bad sitcom she'd co-starred in as a teenager ("All teenagers go through phases. Are you telling me you didn't have a sitcom stardom phase?"), but those deflection strategies only worked when you first accepted your interlocutor's premise. Here, however, she couldn't do that. After all, if Bertram was able to later identify her, correctly identify her, then she was as good as jailed. So she could only deny. And there was no smooth way to flatly deny something, never any grace to it. All she could do was offer a blunt denial and a quick pivot.

"Where can I fax the pages?" she asked, looking between

Bertram and Ethan, eager to loop the kid back into it. "Do you have a home fax?"

"Oh," Bertram said. "Yes." He swayed a bit; the rigid posture of certainty from a moment ago had just given way.

"Dad, that's for Mom's work. She doesn't like it when we—"

"It's our home fax," Bertram said, rooting through his wallet for a card.

"So," Bridget said, giving Ethan her full attention. "When you get the scene, you'll be reading for Anakin, and the most important thing to keep in mind is what you want in the scene. Your motivation drives everything."

"Exactly," Bertram said, handing over a business card. *Eileen Cline, Agribusiness Consulting*. He continued: "Motivation. It's like I always say: You can't self-actualize until you self-factualize."

Bridget knew that anyone who cited themselves as a source of wisdom was an ideal mark.

"Did you come up with that?" she said, touching Bertram's forearm.

"Well, I—"

A few minutes later, when Bridget met Jake back behind a brutalist arrangement of hay bales, he quickly sat down, crossed his legs.

He said, "Yeah?"

"It's a go," she said. "We have to find a fax machine quick." She gestured for him to get up.

"Just let me relax for like a second." He stared at the ground.

So much of the time they wasted was Bridget just waiting for Ethan's boner to drop. "No rush," she said.

They found a Kinko's in a strip mall that seemed in the gradual process of either revitalization or deterioration; she couldn't quite tell the vector. Bridget took the Trapper Keeper from the trunk of her car, the Trapper Keeper in which she kept the three scenes she'd written for an imaginary *Star Wars* script, and in the Kinko's she faxed them over to the home of an agribusiness consultant.

She took an odd pride in those pages, both in the ventriloquism required in their composition—the intentionally stiff dialogue, clotted with terms studiously acquired—and in the ways she painstakingly made them look xeroxed from a complete script, a final scrap of a previous scene visible at the top of one page, the start of another scene visible at the bottom of another. It was a kind of reverse archeology, crafting something with the sole intent of it being legible, but only partially so, to eyes unfamiliar with the particulars of this subculture and its artifacts. In that project, she drew on her own experience in this business that seemed not so much to build necessary life skills as to actively rob you of them. But now she'd found a clear application for that knowledge.

"Block the return number," she told the Kinko's guy. "Please."

He nodded, feeding the pages into the fax behind the counter.

When she went to the Clines' house two days later, a not-quite ostentatious colonial two-story with his and hers Ford Broncos out front (gendered by the hubcaps, turquoise-inlaid and rhinestone-studded, respectively), she left Jake back at the motel. That was the deal. He couldn't be seen or heard until it was his cue. But she was getting increasingly worried about him being holed up in that motel room while she went to work. He clearly didn't leave the room. What at first she'd taken to be his abundance of caution, she now realized was his abundance of reclusiveness. He was a monk of masturbation, and while she didn't worry about him going blind, she was concerned about what a darkened room lit only by a TV screen was doing to his rods and cones, and what the complete deprivation of peer contact was doing to his development.

This was not a permanent arrangement, she reminded herself, as she was shown through the Clines' suspiciously clean living room, which led into another living room that actually looked lived in, then a dining room, which looped back into the unused living room; this was a house that seemed to have metastasized.

It was Bertram who was giving her the tour, sober now, not stained with grape juice. But where sobriety tempered his bluster, the pride he clearly took in this house—or three houses that had collided into each other—aggravated it.

Bridget was carrying a camcorder, a Panasonic DV Pro, in a plastic case the size of a carry-on. Over her shoulder, she had a tote bag with, among other things, a tripod. She set both onto a couch that looked display-room ready. "This will be great," she said. "The lighting."

As she set up the camera, Bertram said he was off to "get the movie star out of his trailer."

She wondered how Jake was doing at the motel.

She soon heard Ethan in the hallway, asking his dad to stay out of the room while he was doing the scene. He then came in alone, wearing a button-up shirt, his hatred for it palpable. It was a shiny metallic fabric that suggested a parent was trying to find something hip but church-nice for him. That boded well. He was clutching the scenes, the fax pages silky and impossible to keep propped up. She asked him to sit down at the chair she'd placed against a blank white wall, the camera three feet from his face. She asked him how comfortable he was feeling with the scenes, and she guided him into a brief discussion of the character's motivations, conflicts internal and external, her voice practiced in the way it presented emotional abstractions as concrete and accessible, as if she were just asking Ethan to assemble a model airplane.

"Let's just run through it a few times," she said. "You got this. Just breathe. Your body takes care of the rest."

She turned on the camera. He didn't seem to notice. She'd placed a strip of black electrical tape over the red recording light, so as to not spook kids like Ethan. She read the other character, Obi-Wan. It was a scene in which the mentee stood up to his mentor for the first time, and off camera, over the course of three read-throughs, Bridget coaxed flashes of anger from Ethan. This ultimately wasn't important for the scene; after all, the tape she was making wasn't going anywhere. But it was important for Ethan to feel like he'd really done something there, that he'd tapped into reserves of emotion that could be seen, validated, monetized. She sometimes wondered why she even bothered with the tape, but it seemed somehow important. She needed it for herself, not for them. The weight of the camera, the sound of the tape spooling through the gears.

When it was done, Ethan relaxed, a new confidence settling over him.

"That's it?" he said.

"That's it," she said. "I'll FedEx the tape this afternoon."

"To Hollywood?"

"Marin County."

Bertram entered with a glass of wine. He held the stem of the glass in his fist.

The parents always wanted her to stay, to socialize. With the burden of the audition tape out of the way, they wanted to ply her with wine and get insider industry gossip. They wanted to be able to tell people that they had secondhand information about the proclivities of movie stars and studio heads. They wanted to know about Richard Gere's gerbil, wanted themselves to burrow into the strange unlit caverns of the elite, but they always went about it elliptically, and only after opening a second bottle.

She hated this part. But it was necessary. It was necessary to accept a glass of wine from a flush-faced father. It was necessary to offer coy little scraps of gossip that sounded just plausible enough. It was necessary to demystify the process while still keeping it, essentially, mysterious. It was necessary to make them feel like they had a hand guiding them through what was to come.

It was also necessary for her to preface these post-taping sessions with "I'll FedEx the tape this afternoon." That was her escape hatch, an urgency they both understood and invested in.

By the time she gestured to her recording equipment, Bertram's gesticulations were beginning to look like he was doing semaphore. "Yes, yes," he was saying, "go, go, of course, of course," providing his own echo.

After she left, after she went back to the motel and ordered pizza for dinner (pizza was for the tentative celebration; when they really celebrated, when the whole job was done, then she splurged for pay-per-view), after all that, they had to wait—days, a week, more. That was hard. It was especially hard for Jake, who needed to play the next part. But that somehow made it easier for Bridget; having to manage Jake's restlessness gave her something to do with her own.

Until, four days later: "Okay," she said. "Do it."

"You sure?"

"I'm sure."

Sitting in that same motel room that had begun to acquire the fug of fast food and towels left too long on the bathroom floor, Jake did his vocal warm-ups. Scales and breathing. These were not warm-ups Bridget had shown him intentionally, but ones he'd seen her do when gripped by anxiety. When she'd first seen him do these warm-ups, she'd assumed he was mocking her. But then she was heartened to see that he'd clearly understood the value of something that brought you back into your body when gravitational forces of a world gone mad threatened to remove you from it.

Bridget dialed the number and handed Jake the phone. He held his chest while it was ringing, and Bridget said, "Breathe. Your body takes care of—"

Something flashed across Jakes' face—someone picked up—and he launched into the script, about how he was calling from Vernum School, about how he'd received their contact information from the coordinator at LucasFilm, and that if they needed Ethan enrolled for high school credits for the spring semester, they needed to act soon. He paused. Then, affecting the annoyance of a functionary with a deadline and too many responsibilities, he explained how Vernum was a non-public school that the studio contracts with to ensure child performers get a premium on-set education that accommodates the demands of any filming schedule and that they are regionally accredited. And—yes, he was just calling because he was given their contact information and told the start date is January tenth, so he would assume Ethan Cline had a role, but he didn't have any information other than that, but what was most important, the reason he was calling, was that if they wanted Ethan enrolled for the spring semester, and if he didn't want to lose any high school credits, a loss which would delay his graduation, the school needed the tuition deposit, which was usually refunded by the studio, but which was due tomorrow, by money order. And sure, there were other options, but coordinating with the local school districts was a process that often left student actors credit deficient, whereas Vernum had fostered young talents all the way to the Ivy League, and he really needed to know if Ethan would be joining them for the spring semester.

Jake was talking impressively fast. So much of their success depended on the precise ways she and Jake dilated and contracted time; speed things up to excite them, then slow things down to let disappointment creep in, and then speed things up again, faster now, beyond anyone's ability to think.

Jake looked at Bridget. His eyes widened almost imperceptibly, and he said, "I'll express you the Vernum literature along with a return envelope tonight."

Jake allowed himself only one celebratory fist pump before he hopped off the bed and got into his navy-blue jumpsuit with the generic *express* patch ironed onto the breast. He took the manila envelope, which contained the Vernum brochure Bridget made last year, and an envelope pre-addressed to the P.O. box out in Springston, the Vernum regional office.

"Drive safe," she said.

"You too," he said, heading out.

"Ha ha," she said, after he'd closed the door.

Bridget immediately fielded a call from Bertram on her cell phone. Sorry, she explained, she'd been trying to get ahold of him forever, but she could see from the caller ID on her cell that she must have been transposing the one and the three in his number. And yes, they want Ethan out there as soon as possible. The coordinator from LucasFilm should be in touch with them, so she'll follow up with them tomorrow and get everything squared away. And yes, she'd heard of Vernum, great teachers, LucasFilm reimburses, and they're the ones who helped Brooke Shields get into Princeton, so she'll reach out to the coordinator at LucasFilm and then they'll be in touch about everything. Really, they're so good at making this process as smooth as possible for families. "Give my biggest congrats to Ethan!"

Once Jake got to the Clines' neighborhood, he'd park a few blocks away, as they surely saw Bridget's car when she'd come to tape the audition, and he'd rush up to their door, drop the envelope on the welcome mat, knock three quick times and leave.

Meanwhile, Bridget would set to work on her cell phone. It was shockingly simple to reset it herself, to anonymize it from the phone number with which she'd committed fraud. This was a skill she'd acquired from the logorrheic proprietor of a pawn shop whose mind was just as cluttered as his store: for every thousand pieces of useless junk, there was one piece of miraculously practical use.

And even then, after Jake came back sweaty from his delivery, even then it wasn't yet time to really celebrate. It was only time to really celebrate when, the following day, Bridget checked the P.O. box and pulled from it an envelope containing the Clines' deposit for Ethan's spring semester at Vernum School.

Using the mail made it a federal crime, but the brochure in that envelope listed different contact information than this P.O. box, so chances were good that they wouldn't be tracked down here, to this sad little post office in a strip mall where Jake waited in the car until Bridget emerged triumphant, envelope in one hand, P.O. box key twirling in the other.

● **REC**

The image wobbles to the rhythm of walking. Through a doorway, faces greet you like an old friend. One approaches and attempts to eat you. The image blurs at the eater's uvula. In a moment, after things refocus, another person smiles, then demonstrates the interior of his nostril, offering a sudden spelunking. The image wobbles past him, onward down a hallway.

3.

But the way it worked over in Claymont wasn't the way it worked here at the Foothill Square Mall, which is to say: "It didn't work."

"Yes, Jake, I know it didn't work."

In fact, even when they got all the way to Jake's delivery, even then it only worked one out of three times.

Three-fourths of all proceeds she wired back to Denver.

From their failure at the Gap, they walked toward the Nordstrom's, beyond which was the lot where they'd parked. She always figured after one failed overture, this mall was spent. Couldn't risk making the same appeal to someone who might then speak to that kid and his mom back in the Gap. In fact, they should have considered the whole town spent. If Bridget were as disciplined as Zig Ziglar told her she needed to be, she would be putting more distance between jobs, would be splurging on more gas money before finding a new mark. And yet, here they were, just barely outside of Claymont because Jake had insisted on this particular mall that didn't even have a proper Bath & Body Works—it had instead some sort of knock-off place called, bafflingly, Cucumber Sunglasses. Aside from the actual sunglasses made to look like cucumber slices that they sold on a standee by the entrance, Cucumber Sunglasses stayed firmly within the scented soap lane. It was an olfactory assault, and Bridget loved it.

"I'm not going in there," Jake said.

"So don't. Wait over in the arcade."

He grunted and dragged himself across the way to that small arcade with carpet like a neon Jackson Pollack design.

Inside Cucumber Sunglasses, she calmed herself with pamplemousse bath candles and soaps carved like little seashells. Those tallowy textures gave just enough resistance in her hand that when she pushed a thumbnail in, leaving a little crescent wound, it was like pressing her hand into wet cement outside Mann's Chinese Theater. An imprint left for posterity. She imagined all those famous handprints being visible to the alien archaeologists who'd sift through the remains of the nuclear-blasted hellscape of the future. Her thumbnail mark in a mauve-colored soap surely wouldn't last, but it still felt satisfying. She slid the soap into her pocket with one hand, while replacing the candle on the shelf with the other. Bridget then moved to the array of face scrubs, little clear plastic pouches in which she could see bluish bubbles suspended in goo. Above those, the luffas hung out like arthropod fossils. Tactically, this one was both smooth and rough, a reminder that abrasion was not simply a matter of material, but a matter of force, what you did with it.

"You like?" This voice belonged to a woman beside her. She was young, her face matted by anxious foundation.

"Yes," Bridget said, looking for another shelf of exotic exfoliants to shuffle off to.

"Try this one." The woman picked up the luffa Bridget had been touching. "It's the best one." She was wearing the seafoam green button-up of a store employee. She had a nametag, but it was blank. She held the luffa out to Bridget, but Bridget didn't take it. She grabbed Bridget's hand and put the luffa in her palm. Bridget pulled her hand away but was now holding the luffa.

"Here," the woman said. "This." She picked up a pumice stone roughly the shape of Iowa. "It's not the best, but it's my favorite. Has a good weight to it." She reached for Bridget's other hand, but this time Bridget angled away. The woman suddenly put the pumice stone into the side pocket of Bridget's canvas jacket. "Take it."

Bridget tried to put the luffa back on the shelf, but the woman blocked her, pushed the product back to Bridget's chest.

"You like taking things, so just take it, okay?"

This woman with a blank name tag was clearly insane, and she was now reaching for other items on the shelf to shove into Bridget's thieving possession.

Bridget stumbled back, looked around for help. They were the only ones in the store.

"There's more," the woman said, grabbing a bottle of what looked like shelf-stable strawberry milkshake.

But Bridget got out of there.

She was all the way to the Orange Julius before she stopped to look back, make sure that Cucumber Sunglasses girl wasn't following her to douse her in lye and mold her remains into heart-shaped hand soap.

"Jesus Christ," she muttered, discovering that in addition to the pumice stone still in her pocket, she had a pair of pink eyebrow tweezers. Leaving the stone in her pocket like a suburban Virginia Woolf, she sat on the side of a bench and idly poked the pad of her finger with the tweezers. She could see the entrance to the arcade from here, imagined Jake was enjoying his moment of pretending to be normal.

She found a bathroom and waited until she was sure the stalls were empty, that she was alone, and she leaned over the counter, her face close to the Windex-streaked mirror, and examined her eyebrows. The little hairs that drifted from the herd needed to go. She tweezed each with a precision that was almost as satisfying as the little pings of pain. Of the two tools she'd unwillingly pilfered, the tweezers and the pumice stone, the former was more her jam: exacting and sharp, rewarding a steady hand and tolerance for pain that was precise. The latter tool was too blunt for her taste, requiring a grunting strength and ability to withstand the attritional mode of beauty. When she was young, leaning as close to the mirror as she could before her eyes lost focus, she extracted blackheads between her fingernails with a joy that anticipated her later sexual experiments. The fact that she performed those little self-harvesting rituals in the tiny bathroom of her trailer on the set of *In a Pickle* made it all the more thrilling: knowing that she couldn't leave any nail-crescent wounds on her nose for the makeup artist to scold her for. In college, when she was putting off the inevitability of Tod, she briefly dated a man who was an aspirant to the tug-of-war championship she hadn't known existed. In order to remain competitive, in addition to strange exercises that targeted muscle groups that sounded like dinosaurs, he needed to build up the calluses on his hands, so he had a special brick that he rubbed his palms against. For hours, while watching TV, he'd grind his palms against that rough red brick until all tenderness had turned to carapace. "It's about controlling the body, babe," he said. "So it doesn't control you."

Three eyebrow hairs lighter, Bridget emerged from the bathroom, back into the mall festooned with plastic ferns draped with orange and black streamers. The dirt in which these plastic ferns had been stuck was wormed with the desiccated bits of Silly String, similarly Halloween-colored. Above her, inflatable mylar ghosts lingered in the middle strata of the mall's air space, having lost just enough helium to no longer cling to the windowed ceiling, while retaining just enough to float out of arm's reach, kids periodically jumping to try and grab one. These specters were far spookier than their fully inflated forms could have been.

She sat on the wide edge of the tiled planter. It was cold through her pants. She rubbed her hands against the mortar between the tiles, then looked at her palms, the play of lines. Maybe that college boyfriend had been right; maybe the trick was insulating yourself from the world, not assimilating into it, that flesh was meant to be hardened, not bleed. When Jake and Mabel were in the same fourth grade class, Jake would occasionally come home with a fine dry gloss over his fingertips. When she asked about it, he explained that it was super glue, that during some crafts project he'd applied a thin layer of the liquid adhesive to each fingertip. "It's gross," Mabel said. "While we're trying to clean up, he's taking off his fingerprints like a serial killer." Jake held up his ten glossy fingers and said, "She's right. Not for serial killing, but it is good for crimes."

She figured it was time to go get Jake, to get him out of the arcade, out of the mall, and back on the road. They needed to put more distance between themselves and Claymont. Approaching the arcade, the freakout of the tinny blooping music got louder, more spastic.

Inside, she was saddened to not recognize the games. She'd hoped for something that pinged a familiar neuron, but this new generation of games was assaultive and disorienting, eager to disabuse her of any notion that she could navigate the terrifying media of the new youth.

There, tiptoeing up to some sort of shooting game, was a small boy, about eight or nine, about the age when Jake was supergluing the fingerprints from his skin. This boy even had that same floppy haircut Jake used to have, an emerging flaxen bob beneath which a little V of freshly trimmed hair connected head to nape. She had the urge to squeeze his shoulders, to give him a kiss on his head. She didn't, of course. She knew this was not Jake, that this was not eight years ago, that if she did give this boy a kiss on his head, it wouldn't smell the same, and his real mother would soon enter stage right with a left hook. She smiled, felt stupid about her smile, clenched it.

"Sarah." It was Jake—the real one—coming up behind her. He tapped her on the shoulder. He'd never done that before.

"What?" she said. "Why are you calling me that name?"

"Sarah, let me introduce you to someone."

Jake moved slightly to reveal a boy, about his age, standing just behind him.

"This," Jake said, "is Caleb."

Caleb slouched like an asshole. He'd clearly bought his pants in the big and tall section, and the way they flared out completely obscured his feet. But he had the right look, the way he quietly demanded the space he occupied. The kid came from money, and now he came to her.

"Hello, Caleb," she said. "You look familiar."

But why had Jake brought him to her? Why had he strayed from protocol? They had a clear system, a system that worked, and as soon as he got his part down he was trying to mix things up?

"That's what I thought," Jake said. "But he's never done any camera work, none at all."

"Oh." She leaned back a bit, as if to take him all in. "Well, that's a shame."

Caleb tucked his hands into his pockets, an ineffectual gesture of nonchalance, since his pants were too low to hold more than his fingertips. "But I've been thinking I should get some sort of modeling agent. He said that." Caleb nodded at Jake. "People say I should do that all the time."

Usually, when dealing with kids like Caleb, kids whose sense of their masculine identity seemed too performative to be stable, she stayed away from any suggestion that what she was offering them was in any way playacting, could in any way be perceived as something feminine. Instead of mentioning makeup and costumes and playing pretend for the camera, she emphasized the elements that appealed to the young method-aspirant: desire and conflict. But here Jake seemed to have gone and tossed the idea of modeling into the mix, and—even more shocking—Caleb was down for it.

The youth, she thought—as she outlined for Caleb the parameters of the *Star Wars* project and her role in finding George Lucas's teenage Vader—continued to surprise her.

And the surprises continued.

"So you got him into a TV show?" Caleb said, nodding at Jake.

Jake had apparently introduced a backstory she would have to figure out on the fly. The kid turned sixteen, passed the GED, and suddenly decided to start improvising.

"That's right," she said. "He can tell you all about it."

And as she guided the two teenage boys out of the arcade to have a seat by the Orange Julius, Jake—whose name, according to Caleb, was Ryan—did just that, told Caleb about how it was called a pilot, and how easy and fun it was to hang out on a set all day, to get your own trailer, scripts delivered to you in big envelopes. It was unclear what sort of show Ryan had been in, or if this pilot had been picked up by the network, but it didn't really matter. Caleb wasn't asking questions; he was only offering declaratives, assuming that whatever Bridget—or rather, Sarah—was offering was already his.

"I don't do nude scenes," he said, his brow affecting a thoughtful scrunch, like Clinton performing compassion for a press conference.

"Of course," Bridget said, making sure that he knew she was taking this idiotic concern seriously. "These films are going to be PG. No swearing. A little violence, sure, but no gore. And no nudity."

"Unless it's right for the character," Caleb said thoughtfully.

"Well," Bridget said, "I don't think it would be. Anakin, that's Vader's real name, he's not really the type to, you know. After all, he's famous for his mask, right? For his armor?"

"That armor is sick," Caleb said.

"Made of durasteel," Jake said.

Bridget was taken aback by this little interjection. She tried to nudge Jake's leg under the table but just wound up kicking at empty space and needing to adjust her position to cover for her little spasm.

"So with all that armor," she continued, "he's the kind of guy who is very protective of himself, and characters like that don't tend to have nude scenes."

Caleb seemed unimpressed by this nugget of fool's gold.

"All that armor," Jake said. "He's hiding something."

"Yeah," Caleb said, nodding to his peer. "Really messed up stuff."

"Exactly," Jake said.

"Like gnarly burns and sores and stuff."

"Nah," Jake said, mirroring Caleb's inflection. "Secrets."

Caleb nodded, squinted his eyes. "Gotcha."

Jake was, somehow, better at luring Caleb than she was,

and she knew she should just let him show her what he could do here, but she couldn't. "So it's up to you," she said to Caleb, "to make a choice about what those secrets are. Because the camera sees that."

Caleb looked from Jake to Bridget and, after wiping the tip of his nose, said, "I always wondered if he had a robot dick."

"Maybe he does." Bridget, unsure if he was serious or messing with her, tried to keep her response neutral and then pivoted: "Let's get your picture." She pulled from her tote bag the Polaroid camera, along with an index card and a Bic pen. "This is called a contact card," she said, pushing the pen and index card toward him. "Name, phone number, height, weight, hair color, eye color. You're going to need to hook a fax machine up to the number. That's how we'll get the sides to you. Sorry, that's what we call the scenes that you'll be performing. Will you be able to do that?"

Already filling out the contact card, Caleb said, "We got a separate fax line."

With Caleb's gaze averted, she shot a look at Jake. Jake, however, was just idly scanning the rest of the mall, nodding to some song in his head.

"Perfect," Bridget said when Caleb slid the completed card over to her. "Now"—holding up the Polaroid camera—"smile."

"No." Caleb stood up and walked away.

Bridget exhaled, leaned her elbows on the table. Disappointment never got easier to digest; it just came in different flavors.

"Over here." It was Caleb's voice. He was leaning against the wall, one foot propped up, knee out. He crossed his arms. "Like this."

Bridget rushed over to him. She heard Jake follow.

"With the wall," Caleb said, "it'll look more like a mug

shot, but like I'm still chill about it."

"I *love* it," Bridget said. She took the picture, noting to herself that he did look kind of cool, and then hating herself for thinking that.

Later, after they'd parted with Caleb, having said they'd fax over the sides for three scenes and that they'd be in touch about when they could come over and put him on tape, after Jake did some sort of fist bump with Caleb and after they watched him saunter away, after she was sure Caleb was out of sight and earshot, she slugged her son on the arm.

She said, "What the hell?"

"What?"

"You're going fishing on your own now?"

"What do you think you've been preparing me for this whole time? It's like you say: Success is when opportunity meets preparation."

"That's not me. That's Zig Ziglar." They only had three cassette tapes in the car, and on long stretches of road, when they tired of *The Big Chill* soundtrack and *The Very Best of Linda Ronstadt*, they'd listen to Zig Ziglar spew bon mots about the mindset of thriving. "And you're not prepared. Prepared isn't just making stuff up."

"Improvising."

"Prepared isn't just throwing me in there without warning."

"But it worked. We did our things perfectly."

They were making their way through Nordstrom's, past the glass counters of watches, through the autumnal displays of medium-weight jackets.

"You already have a thing! What are we gonna do about that, huh?"

"I'm tired of just being a dipshit in a delivery jumpsuit."

They passed by mannequins in various stages of dress,

toward the shoe racks by the doors that led out into the parking lot.

"Is that what this is about?"

"I want stuff to do."

"You had stuff to do."

"Why are you angry? It worked!"

"Not yet, it hasn't. It all rests on the parents. And we haven't met the parents yet. Haven't met—" Now in the afternoon sun of the parking lot, she looked at the contact card that she'd paperclipped to the Polaroid of Caleb Docter. "Haven't met Mr. and Mrs. Docter yet."

"They sound like money," he said.

"E-R," she said, "not O-R."

"What do you mean? That they're like emergency room doctors, not operating room?"

"That's how they spell it, their name. Docter with an E-R."

"That's stupid."

She was scanning the gleaming rooftops of the cars, couldn't see the blight of rust that marked the roof of their Camry. "Where are we?"

"I did a good job," Jake said.

"We're in the wrong lot."

"I picked a good one. I did exactly what you wanted."

"How'd we get in the wrong lot?"

"I did a good job."

"How did I get here?"

● **REC**

Hands, fingernails scabbed and flecked green, straightening something. Pulling back, you can see the edges of a black sheet. Fingers affix its border with thumbtacks—to a wall, perhaps. Pushing in, closer to the work of the hands and the tacks and the black sheet, the image starts to blur and, with a verbal invitation to get fucked, the hand swats at you.

4.

How did she get here? The question wasn't quite right, the suggestion of arrival when in fact hers was a story of departure. The *here* was not a specific point in time and space; it was any place that wasn't *there*, there being her home—her and Jake's home—back in Denver. Wherever she happened to be was not so much here as not there.

In Denver there was a house, a nice house: that's what they'd said, they'd all said. That it was nice. The realtor and the rest, sundry family members who decided to visit with minimal warning because they'd heard tell of available guest rooms. That the house was *so nice*. Newly made, in a subdivision that was *safe*. She and Tod had picked the house from a binder of options—house A, house B, house C, and so on—as-is or hybridizing the parts; a Doric column from A, a mansard window from C. Those weren't the names, of course. The houses had actual names that sounded like Thomas Kinkade paintings: Autumn Reach and Wisteria Manor. But to Bridget, they were more readily identifiable by the bold, blunt letters in the upper right-hand corners of the binder pages in which they were so lewdly splayed. When finished, their house had all the things it needed, as if from a Lego set. The house was *nice*.

In the house in Denver was a man, a *nice* man: that's what they'd said, they'd all said. And he was. Tod was nice. So nice he somehow got away with having only one *d* in his name. Maybe because his parents didn't name him Theodore. On the birth certificate, they named him the diminutive, and then decided to make it even more diminutive by lopping off that superfluous *d*. No, Tod wasn't Todd; he wasn't descended from a line of gentry who shopped at shoppes. Tod was from the flatlands of Kansas, and the bluntness of his name—almost onomatopoetic in the way it sounded like the impact of his shin on the edge of the coffee table—spoke to the directness of his people. Directness was his family's way of assimilating occasional flashes of being *not nice* into their general vibe of *niceness*. And Tod was nice. Organizing conferences for educational non-profits, he interfaced with a lot of people and had developed a patina of charm just vague enough to be effective but forgettable. It was a charm that Bridget noticed he laced into the way he interacted—or interfaced?—with her in the years between the first mistake and the crash of everything, when she was vigilant for all the ways he might be on to her and her failings.

But in the nice house with the nice man—in which all the pieces fit just so—there was a missing puzzle piece. Specifically, it was about seven square feet of space on the second floor that could not accommodate Bridget and Tod's selection of walk-in closet 7B with master bedroom number 5H. It was a small trapezoid of space that could not be integrated into the closet, bedroom, or hallway, windowless and big enough for only one person. During construction the developer suggested it could become a vanity room. "A space," the man explained, "adjacent to where one does one's toilet, primarily for doing one's makeup before a confluence of mirrors." Bridget and Tod agreed mostly because it seemed like the only realistic option for that leftover space and because the developer seemed weirdly stoked to do it. Maybe, Bridget wondered, if a man who made houses was focused daily, hourly, on the function of things, it might be an odd kind of escape to make something that seemed entirely functionless. A little room with mirrors. A cocaine closet, Bridget and Tod joked. Or Bridget joked; it was unclear if Tod heard her. When Bridget finally stepped foot into the vanity room, a week before their official move-in, she was achingly pregnant with Jake and Mabel. The floor was soft with shag; there was a tiny built-in countertop where you could apply makeup before a nauseating arrangement of mirrors. So many small mirrors affixed at slightly varied angles, the whole effect like that of an insect's compound eye. The body that she saw from a myriad of overlit angles—because that one small light reflected back and forth in an infinity of mirror images—was simply enormous. No single mirror could contain the wholeness of her twin-pregnant belly. It appeared in disco-ball shards.

When that belly had been vacated, Jake and Mabel began having their own existentially fraught mirror experiences with each other, as even in infancy their twinship seemed more incidental than identical. Meanwhile, Bridget had replaced that concussion of a light bulb with a dim tea light, powered by a tiny watch battery the size of a baby aspirin. But even that, when reflected in all those mirrors, became dizzying, so she began painting over the mirrors, one by one, with acrylic blues and blacks, the feeling of running a wet brush over a glass surface oddly satisfying, until the only reflective surface that was left unpainted in her vanity room was a single face-high mirror the size and dimensions of a headshot.

As Jake and Mabel began crawling, the first place she taught them they weren't allowed to go was the vanity room. It was where she went to blot things out, to reduce the insistence of the visible world down to a small window of manageable space. "Jesus," Tod said when he returned from his trip to Bloomington or Toledo or wherever he was organizing some conference of lanyard-wearing tryhards. "Being in this room is like being buried alive."

"You said I could do what I wanted with it."

"Just keep the door closed. Creeps me out."

And then he was off again, to Santa Fe or Park City or Tempe. Wherever a hotel conference room had a stack of folding tables, he'd be there; wherever enough middle-management types longed to acquire an extra line on their résumé, he'd be there; wherever people used *network* as a verb, he'd be there.

It was April, the nicest month, Tod had said, and Bridget was alone in that house with two infants. Infants whose needs were broadcast in stereo. Infants whose needs never seemed to make room for the other, much less her. And sure, she loved them, of course—but it was the *of course* that drove her into the dimmed vanity room, the voice in her head that said anything other than pure selflessness must be evidence of a glitch in her soul, evidence that her love wasn't true, that she was a fraud in a mother's stained sweatpants. The babies could deal with a *not now*, but that voice could not. At least Jake and Mabel's needs were mostly concrete, immediately satisfied with the simple offering of a teat—because the suppleness of *breast* and the roundness of *boob* no longer applied to parts of her body that once seemed so crucial to her understanding of self and purpose, but which she now pulled out as if they no longer belonged to her. It was all the other things, the things that creaked abstractly in her brain like the unidentifiable sounds the house made in the night; those were the things, the tasks, the obligations not satisfied in ways immediate and bodily that drove her to finally cover that last square of mirror with a dark indigo. If only she could cross everything else off her list in the same way, the list that was in her handwriting but had been dictated by Tod the day before he left for Scranton or Indianapolis; if only she could schedule that meeting with the local HOA by wiping the mustardy poo from their butt; if only she could make those changes to their homeowner's insurance by blending up an avocado and spooning it into their gummy mouth; if only she could finish filing last year's taxes by cranking up the white noise machine and humming dimly remembered lullabies.

In a mall bookstore where she took the babies because the store had a well-padded kids' corner and employees too stoned to care, she read about task management, how President Eisenhower developed a simple yet ingenious design for his to-do lists: four quadrants that triaged obligations from urgent to the noncritical: do, decide, delegate, delete. It was a system she quickly adopted herself, in part because of the liberatory power of that *delete* quadrant. But inside Bridget's mind, the borders between the quadrants became porous, and things she could have sworn she'd placed in the *do* box somehow wound up in the *decide* box, then in the *delegate* box, until finally they'd found a permanent home in the *delete* box, attic of the uncritical. It wasn't so much a choice to shuffle "finish taxes" into the *delete* box, but that's where she found it when Tod called her and asked if she'd done the taxes. The thing about the Eisenhower Box is that the definition of urgent is not universal. One person's *do* is another's *delete*, and you can't tell a guy like Tod, a guy who not only flossed but had a preferred brand of floss, that task-urgency was a relative concept. She lived not only in his house (he always identified it as such), but in his Eisenhower Box. So she said yes, she'd done it. And she would do it, soon, before he came back. A few days late wouldn't matter. She could blame the mail; it was always slow. But the *delete* box had a gravity all its own. Once something entered its atmosphere, it was nearly impossible for it to leave.

Time passed and no black-suited G-men kicked down their door, that door with the little frosted-glass window panel that Tod had paid extra for; time passed and the babies grew, and she entered new stages of parental awareness and vigilance, from tracking the viscosity of poos to marking hand-eye co-ordination across the midline; time passed, and Tod came and went, his returns home from business trips making him seem increasingly like he was a guest; time passed, and there were only a few envelopes from the IRS that she scuttled, less from Tod's awareness than her own, as the anxiety of that transgression—if inaction can ever be transgressive—fizzed at the periphery of her consciousness like distortion on a VHS taped over too many times.

Tod lived up to his promise of nice. When she'd met him at college in Boulder—paid for by her brief but profitable stint on *In a Pickle*, or at least what was left after she'd had to sue her parents for trying to take everything—she marked Tod immediately as the kind of guy you'd be stupid not to marry. His face was symmetrical and he spoke in full sentences. He rode a bike around campus and wore a helmet. He smelled like Dove soap and tutored at a nearby middle school. In Western Philosophy, he spoke like someone who'd done the reading, not like someone trying to prove they'd done the reading. And the sleeves of that softball shirt he sometimes wore hugged the crooks of his biceps in pleasing ways. And that's all why she'd kept him away until the end of senior year, when she could better convince herself that she'd gotten all that other stuff out of the way. Point being, though, he satisfied those tacit promises: he had a good income and, when he was in town, he was patient and attentive with Jake and Mabel. When one of them—the girl, maybe—vomited on his shirt a minute before he had to rush out the door, he was able to change quickly without anger. His equanimity felt oddly accusatory, Bridget acutely aware that she would have lost it. She looked for moments when he could snap too. From her dark hiding spot in the vanity room, which shared a wall with the twins' room, she could dimly listen to him read *Goodnight Moon* to them, listen to his voice calmingly litanize and bid farewell to the artifacts of the waking world. In that particular voyeuristic moment she didn't find what she'd been looking for, didn't find evidence that he was human too, but she found something that pulled her into a sleep from which she awoke hours later on the soft shag floor of the vanity, cramped and cold.

The twins were walking by the time Tod flew back to his April conference. Just before leaving, he'd given a farewell reminder for her to take care of the taxes. The twins walking meant that the territory of what needed childproofing expanded exponentially. Life was organized into things okay for them to grab, to chew, to poke into the other's face, and things not okay to grab, to chew, to poke into the other's face. To go through the day was to catalog and re-catalog every item—every comb, every brush, every bowl full of mush, not to mention every knife, every pin, every bottle full of gin—that constructed their life, assessing it for where it landed on the harm index. When every single piece of matter needed such attention, it was impossible for her to create any economy of perception; all details were equally important, which meant that no one detail was more important. The four quadrants of the Eisenhower Box collapsed into a pile of panic.

She was now good at policing the mail, like some Soviet censor, to make sure nothing unapproved made its way to Tod.

IRS envelopes were easy to spot. She kept a brown paper bag hidden behind the bookless bookshelf in the foyer, and that's where she'd quickly stash the *urgent* envelopes to be torn to pieces later, often at night in the garage.

By the time the twins were in kindergarten, she was taking care of it. Because there was no hiding it for this long, she was taking care of it. Because it was just a simple mix-up at the IRS, she was taking care of it. Because it was surely just a matter of getting the right person on the phone who could confirm that she'd paid the last five years of taxes, she was taking care of it.

That was her role, her job. He didn't need her help with his job, so she didn't ask for help with hers. She was taking care of it.

That's what everyone else was doing, taking care of their own shit. All those moms and dads organizing the Westlake Elementary Talent Show ("WETS?" "Yes"), they were all taking care of their own shit. They didn't ask for help; they asked for participation. Could she participate? Could she make the donation of her time? Could she help build community? She had, after all, such experience in the performing arts. This from a man named Wendell, a father of Jake and Mabel's classmate, a man whose jowls bore the heaviness of alcoholic bloat but whose energy seemed eager to compensate. He'd done his homework on her, something vaguely predatory about the way he knew about her televised past. But it worked, and in no time she was working alongside all those other PTA members who so effortlessly seemed capable of taking care of their own shit. They were all lovely people who surely didn't have coffin-like rooms in their nice houses devoted to darkness and solitude. When Wendell realized that the PTA's credit card had an erroneous charge on it from a local department store, she watched him just call up customer service and report the problem and just like that it was taken care of—the charge evaporated. Wendell hadn't perseverated over the task, hadn't announced to the others that the world was designed to destroy him, as Bridget routinely announced to her two five-year-olds; he just picked up the phone, said there'd been a mistake, that the card had been compromised, and that was that. Problem over. People taking care of their own shit.

Her card arrived the day of the talent show. As she escorted kids in their magician costumes to their places backstage, she had the envelope in her purse, unopened, where she could reach in and touch it, the rigid rectangle of the card offering reassurance. When a third grader who'd signed up to perform "Tomorrow" from *Annie* began to have a panic attack, she crouched down to the girl's level, held her gently but firmly by the shoulders, and said, "You got this. Just breathe. Your body takes care of the rest." These were words the on-set coach had always said on *In a Pickle*, words she no longer believed—she knew very well that the kid could freeze up like a jacklighted deer, fall off the stage, split her head open, eat through a straw for the rest of her life. But those words were sadly effective at shoring up the spirits of this little girl. "Trust me," Bridget said, "I used to do this." And as that little girl belted out a pitchy "the sun'll come out to-mor-row!" Bridget finally tore open the envelope and held the card, rubbed the pads of her thumbs over the embossed numbers.

And sure the IRS took credit cards, why wouldn't they? They were hip to this, surely. And by the time she was calling to say there'd been an erroneous charge on a credit card that had mysteriously been taken out in her name, she already had another two cards approved and on their way. It was simple. She was taking care of her own shit, and it felt good. That feeling of confidence which now buoyed her might have actually been simple lightheadedness, the way the fear and adrenaline drained the blood from her with vampiric efficiency, but whatever it was it was something different from the leaden cloak of depression that had been draped over her shoulders for years. She began fucking Tod more.

She just had to stay ahead of it, that was all. Like the painkillers she took when recovering from the C-section: she just had to anticipate the pain lurking out there and be proactive about it. She found that she was good at that. She knew how to anticipate chaos and failure, to give the mic to her fears, to admit something wicked this way comes; the next step, the hard step, was doing something about it. But now that she had her system, she knew what to do.

And yes, she did have to acknowledge the constant threats to their credit, but that was simple because "the way these identity thieves work is that once they have your information they just keep running you through the same scams," and Tod nodded, grateful that she was able to take care of it, to stay vigilant with their credit reports. "It's just really complicated," she explained to him.

What was actually complicated was that the amount they owed didn't seem to reflect the amount she was paying off, though she couldn't call them up and say she'd paid this so what was going on. So she just had to trust that her system would work out, because it was the only system she had, and the alternative wasn't so much a system as it was complete collapse.

And people like her didn't suffer complete collapse. People like her were hyper-competent, had risen in the PTA ranks to become president and board member of Westlake Elementary, and then Griffin-Dowd Middle School. People like her were active members of their communities who reached out to those less fortunate, those who couldn't afford the resources she had. People like her were no longer horrified when a fellow achiever parent, as they sometimes self-identified, recognized her from *In a Pickle*. People like her were now practiced enough in the social circles of her community—all those circles within circles, like the complex spirographs Jake and Mabel were now too old to stencil in those crazy gyres—to package her past into rehearsed anecdotes, so that even when some curious snoop followed up by asking if she was the one who'd sued her parents for financial mismanagement and become emancipated at age sixteen, just as the show was canceled, she deployed the right combo of laugh and throwaway life-is-funny lines to quell further interrogation. You didn't interrogate pillars of the community, after all, even when a friendly tour of her house revealed a darkly painted room the size of a single-prisoner cell. Bridget had learned how to swat away those questions like so many summer gnats, and in no time everyone was back to enjoying their Riesling on the back deck, more curious about the cost of their neighbor's new gazebo than such unsocial questions as Bridget's capacity to captain her own life.

When the collapse came, the G-men didn't wear black suits.

● **REC**

Bodies appear in the frame, moving in collisions but seemingly with a purpose. Framed incidentally, accidentally, their project remains obscured. The frame is static, seems to be at waist-level. In neglect, perhaps left on a tabletop, this perspective transforms from that of intruder to that of voyeur. The image blurs, suddenly, concussively, until it focuses again: a single copper rivet in dark denim.

5.

Jake and Mabel were both at Lamont High School, and working on their freshmen genealogy projects, when they started digging into family history. The end result of this project seemed to be some sort of tree-shaped poster, which they decorated with photocopies of daguerreotypes and little paragraphs about the potato famine.

Bridget said, "Isn't a poster project a little—I dunno—middle schooly?"

"It's good for visual learning," Mabel said.

"And you just hang this up the wall when you're done?"

"We present in front of the whole class, and the class asks questions." Mabel was combing her hair in the bathroom mirror, Bridget leaning in the doorway. Mabel was fixating on getting her part straight. When she was little, learning to write, if she'd mess up even a single letter, she'd either start over on a new sheet of paper, or she'd get an X-Acto knife and cut the offending error clean out of her page. She seemed to be directing that same energy toward her hair's uncanny symmetry. Bridget knew this was something she should be worrying about more, but so far it mostly manifested in areas where Mabel earned praise: school, extracurriculars. "Speaking and listening," Mabel said, "is a quarter of the grade."

"You're going to present our whole family history to your peers?" Air it all to their classmates, to the children whose parents Bridget had to see and socialize with?

"I have a worksheet about family history. Jake'll have the same worksheet. All freshmen have to do it. But he'll need help."

Mabel affected a snide tone and Bridget knew she should say something about that tone but she also knew Mabel was right: Jake would need help that Mabel never would. Good on her and all, but Bridget didn't trust what straight-A Mabel would unearth if left to do her own research. Jake's helplessness, on the other hand, at least meant that she could curate a world for him that did not have to involve her parents, who might very well still be alive and not, as she'd insinuated over the years, quite dead. If anyone was going to dig up those bones and discover those bones were actually still-living appendages attached to sentient people who'd never met their grandkids, it was Mabel.

That night, she sat down with Jake and his worksheet. It had clearly been xeroxed countless times over the last decade or more, the lines and letters like those on an ancient map. On those lines, Jake printed his name, then asked, "Where'd we come from?" his nubby pencil poised.

"The usual," Bridget said. "British Isles."

Jake wrote that down, *British Aisles*.

It had been Ms. Rombauer, Jake's third grade teacher, who'd first suggested Jake was stupid, at least compared to Mabel. During a parent-teacher conference, the old, rosewater-smelling church lady had said she'd order tests for Jake and send him into special ed. Bridget put a stop to that, of course, and made sure the school board knew Ms. Rombauer preferred to brand kids as idiots than to teach them.

Bridget now erased Jake's *A* and returned him to the British Isles.

From there, the two of them ranged over the imagined lands of the old country, details vague through the mist, traced the lineage of clans until they converged into houses and then fractured in internecine strife, feudal lords of one century becoming the landed gentry of the next, the occasional crown melted down to decorate the hilt of the knight who must avenge the beheaded potentate.

"Our name," Bridget said. "Got the name from a family of weavers. Obviously."

"Not me. Got my name from Dad."

"Well, Weaver came from a family of actual medieval weavers. Your distaff line was from weavers. Fitting, right? You know what a distaff is?"

Jake was too busy transcribing what she was saying to realize she'd asked him a question.

"It's what gathers the unspun fibers together before they get fed into the spindle." She sipped her tea, chamomile in all its muted dullness.

Jake stopped writing. "I don't think I need this part."

She set down her mug. "One of the Weavers was chased out of her village when human gut was discovered in her weaves. Her loom was burned."

Jake wrote that down. Enough details from the old country and there'd be no room left on the construction paper tree for the slippery details of this country.

"You're spelling 'defenestration' wrong," she told Jake. "Gimme that pencil."

Jake was compliant and had the posture of a paperclip. He seemed oddly disinterested in Bridget's tales of heraldry and betrayal; Jake just dutifully recorded it with the professional remove of a stenographer, a stenographer who misrecorded *serf*—he somehow didn't misspell it as *surf*; that would have been understandable. No, he went with *smurf*, as if his distaff line—now properly labeled as such—had been populated by tiny blue socialists. True, Smurfette and Gargamel might have been just as, if not more, realistic than the nonsense she'd offered him there at their kitchen table, but the credulity of this kid was somehow both precious and terrifying.

She put the pencil back down. She ruffled his hair, felt its unwashed waxiness.

"Why'd you do that?"

"Because I love you."

"Okay." He scratched vigorously behind his ear and said, "I have to do Dad next."

"Oh, they're easy. Kansas. That's all you need to know."

He recorded Kansas on the next page of the packet. "Can you just tell me all his stuff?"

Bridget sipped her mug of tepid tea—it tasted like nothing but was supposed to help her sleep. "Why don't you go talk to him? He'd love to tell you anything you need to know."

Jake was rubbing his face with the heels of his hands. "He just gets frustrated with me."

Bridget took an unsatisfying sip, tried to place the mug back down on the same ring of water it had left on the table. "He just knows how much potential you have, wants you to try hard."

Tod was suddenly in the doorway like an apparition. Jake jerked.

"Ask him," Bridget told Jake.

"Ask me what?" Tod said. He was grinning like a psychopath.

"I have questions for you," Jake said.

"Well, they'll have to wait." He walked to the freezer, pulled out a frozen pizza, tossed it onto the counter where it landed like an errant hubcap. To Jake, Tod said, "You and Mabel are cooking dinner for yourselves tonight. Your mom and I are celebrating."

He held out his hands as if to receive a bounding puppy. Instead Bridget and Jake just blinked at him. "Is this like when you insisted we celebrate Arbor Day?" Bridget asked.

"Yeah," Jake said, "that tree you planted now looks haunted."

Bridget's heart was warmed by Jake roasting his dad.

"Gil," Tod said. "He offered me Executive Director."

Bridget clapped her hands, once. She said: "Great."

She and Tod decided on dinner at Seasonality, a newish place with a fluorescent *organic* sign in the window. They'd been there before, when it opened, and Tod was impressed that the waitstaff offered you pepper from a long wooden grinder, not a shaker in sight. At the time, they were unwowed by the food, but were just touched by the gesture the city seemed to be making.

This time they went for the tasting menu. The waiter left the regular menu on the table, wedged between the candle and the flower vase, so after the first few amuse-bouche they consulted the regular menu and realized that what they'd just eaten was the normal fare chopped into smaller pieces.

Their wine flight came on a flat wooden paddle, and Tod was now telling Bridget this was the exact kind he got spanked with during the hazing for his college rugby team.

"Oh, yeah," she said, smiling. "I remember you telling me. 'Please, sir, may I have another?'"

A passing waiter stopped. "Another wine flight, ma'am? I mean, miss."

"What?" Bridget was almost startled by the waiter's intrusion. "Oh, no."

The waiter excused himself. As soon as he was gone, Bridget let out a laugh.

"I'm sure he'd be willing to paddle us, if we asked," Tod said.

His smile had a dazed patina. "Babe." There was something post-coital about his sigh. "Gil offered it to me when he got back from squash. He was wearing a tank top and he's so—hirsute. Do you think when I can afford his lifestyle, I'll just start sprouting patches of hair on my shoulders?" He looked oddly thrilled by the idea, like at any moment he could turn into a werewolf. "I want to do that add-on to the house. The extra wing on the back for a studio. It'll be amazing. We just have to finally straighten out that credit thing, and we can make it work."

"Sure, babe. You got the golden ticket." She was trying to pace her way down the line of wine glasses. "It's pronounced her-suit."

"I *earned* the golden ticket." He downed the thimble of rosé.

"Not *hair-suit*," she said.

"Save room for dessert. I spotted a salted caramel thing on the menu. It's mine and you're gonna help me with it."

"Once you join the executive class, you might start using words like 'impactful.' I'm not sure I like that. Should we get something else? Like an entrée?"

He said, "You say *her-suit*?"

"We could split the duck." She took the napkin from her lap and leaned down to wedge it under the table's bum leg.

"I've only heard it said *hair-suit*," he said. "Like a suit of hair." He rubbed his temples. "I made an appointment with that tax lawyer. He can help us straighten everything out. Clear out the cobwebs, you know."

"I'm taking care of it," Bridget said. "I told you."

He smiled—ominously or flirtatiously, she couldn't tell. "You did tell me that. In the eighties."

Bridget quickly waved down the waiter, and in a moment he was at the table. Bridget asked him to describe the other wine flight, having a strange fondness for the tactile vocabulary of sommeliers. Flinty, grassy, jammy. Stay, she wanted to tell the waiter, please.

The waiter left, and Bridget had a feeling—perhaps a flinty one—that she was going to be sick.

By the time they returned home from Seasonality, they were both wobbly from the wine.

Pulling into the garage, the windshield bumped the tennis ball hanging on a string from the ceiling; it pendulum-swung back and bounced a few times on the glass while the engine cooled.

"Celebration sex?" Tod said.

"If the kids are asleep."

In the bedroom, they undressed. Tod's posture had improved with his weight gain, as he seemed to have realized that slouching only made his new paunch more pronounced.

In bed, Tod cupped her breast.

She said, "My stomach feels weird. I think that tartare was funny."

"Hmm. It was a little undercooked."

She whispered, "Nighty night, funny man."

She tried to create, with as little movement as possible, a little aura of warmth under the sheets. Still as a sloth, she tried to will herself into sleep. Tod's cold foot touched her bare calf.

"Jesus!" She pulled her legs away from him. "Why?"

"Why what?"

"You're cold as a corpse."

"Warm me."

"No."

When Tod's breathing took on the rhythm of sleep, she slipped out of bed and went into her vanity room, which had over the years acquired a beanbag chair and a little white-noise machine, but not much else. She ran her fingers around one small panel of octagonal mirror, pulled and slid it away to expose a fist-size hole in the drywall. Tucked in there, she found four envelopes, each unopened. She pulled out one, tore it open to find the pre-approved card. She folded the envelope and paperwork into a neat compact square and fit it back into the hole in the drywall, to be disposed of later, and replaced the mirror.

The day Tod set up an appointment with that tax lawyer, to finally straighten things out, Bridget set fire to the bathroom. The appointment was at three. At one-thirty, she went to the bathroom and overwiped. The mountain of toilet paper refused to go gently into that good drain, so she had to plunge and upon coaxing her mess away and out of sight, she lit a candle—jasmine—on the countertop. Finding no multi-surface cleaner below the bathroom sink, she went downstairs to the kitchen, and spent a few extra minutes reorganizing the Pine-Sol and Drano and the dishwashing gloves that were stiff with unidentifiable muck. By the time she returned upstairs she realized two things: First, that she'd forgotten to bring with her the multi-surface cleaner, and second, that there, out of the top of the closed bathroom door, diesel-dark smoke was pouring out and up. It gathered on the ceiling, spreading. She opened the door and smoke plumed out. When it cleared, she could see the hand towel aflame above the jasmine candle, saw that the pink terry cloth had taken hold of that little flame and turned it into a conflagration.

She heard herself shouting about smoke and fire, though it felt more like a soundtrack to her actions than part of them.

She grabbed a bath towel and threw it on the fire. It landed over the candle and towel rack above. For a moment, the fire seemed to calm. The walls were smeared with soot. There must have been a fair amount of plastic in that hand towel.

By the time she heard Tod downstairs, the fire was out. She was wiping the soot from the walls and her face was blacker than a coal miner's. Tod would be angry; he'd tell her they had to go, now, and wouldn't want to hear about the fire that was not her fault, and he'd say something about her looking like a minstrel and why didn't she clean herself up, and either way they'd be late to the appointment with the tax lawyer who was going scalpel into everything.

Already angry at the inconsiderate reaction Tod would have to the crisis she'd heroically faced down herself, she stormed downstairs.

What she found was this: Mabel and Tod sitting at the kitchen table, hunched over a stack of papers, a manila envelope.

Tod looked up at her, his face as unreadable as the runic alphabet. He said some things to her—or maybe asked some things, judging from the inflection. Mabel didn't seem to be saying anything. Her hand was placed on a few papers paperclipped together. She touched them with a sense of ownership. Tod was asking her things, if she knew about some things.

She stepped toward the table, eyed the papers Mabel had gathered. *Internal Revenue Service*, a header read.

She might have asked where they got this.

"You just ask. Besides, FOIA."

That was Mabel speaking, not Tod.

"For your project?" Bridget asked.

"For my project," Mabel said.

"Who's Foya?" Bridget said. "Your friend with the braces?"

"Freedom of Information Act, 1967. Duh."

Tod appeared to be crying. This all seemed to be at a distance, a sense of vertigo—quieting, pacifying—intervening between her and the world.

Bridget asked, "Don't you want to know why I look like this?"

So: When the G-men came, they weren't wearing black suits. They were wearing prestressed jeans and a turtleneck. When they G-men came, they were her own daughter.

After that, it all happened fast: or no, not fast, but the gears felt oiled and rustless, like the machinations of life had been designed, all along, for collapse. It made sense. It had been so much harder keeping things together than it was to just follow along when they fell apart. Entropy was the natural state of things, and her attempts at staving off disorder not only futile but harmful. That first night she slept in her vanity room, curled on the beanbag chair, and it felt like the most natural thing in the world.

Although she and Tod had wound up missing that 3 p.m. appointment with the tax attorney, Tod did eventually meet with him. Bridget didn't go with him; he said it would be best for him to go alone. There were other things that would just be better if she was left out—for now, he said, until things are *clearer*—like that meeting with Jake's school counselor and Mabel's speech and debate fundraiser and a phone call behind a closed bedroom door.

Salvation lay in the details, in the concrete bits of daily life: boiling pasta, folding laundry. When she spoke to her husband, to her daughter, to her son about these things, they looked at her, responded. Everything else, the soft and impressionistic parts of family life, felt removed as if by X-Acto knife, leaving nothing but clean edges.

In this way, as a mere functionary, she could survive. Until she couldn't. Until Tod came to her with the final figure. The number the tax attorney eventually came back to them with didn't seem like it represented a small series of mistakes, but rather a large house or a series of large houses. The sense of injustice flared hot in her chest, but with nowhere to take that she retired to her vanity room, her sensory deprivation chamber. Until even that wasn't enough. Until Tod came to her and said, eyes averted, that he'd checked her into the La Quinta Inn, that it'd just be until they sort all this out, figure out what happened and—his eyes looking into the carpet as if into a Magic Eye poster—what will need to happen next.

The room at the La Quinta Inn had two double beds. The coverlets felt like plastic. The clothes hangers were locked to the rod in the closet. The coffee maker was just big enough for a mug and a half, but there was no mug, just plastic cups that housecleaning didn't replace unless she asked. The towels were too stiff when they were freshly laundered, so she developed a system of rotating towels to always have a slightly used one for her first towel-off, only leaving it on the bathroom floor to be replaced when it had gone through three shower-dries. The window above the rattling air-conditioner didn't open. She asked one of the cleaning ladies about it, but she didn't answer, just smiled and shrugged. "I'm not asking because I want to jump out, by the way," Bridget said. "It just seems like a hazard, is all." The cleaning lady was attending to the sheets with the rigor of someone trying to avoid a woman standing too close and casually mentioning suicide. "Besides," Bridget continued, "this is only the second floor. Motels aren't built for dramatic endings like that. For real splat, you'd have to go to a hotel."

When Jake arrived at her door, she wasn't sure exactly how many days she'd been at the La Quinta Inn, but her son seemed to have aged years, had hefted on pounds that weren't quite fat and weren't quite muscle, just mannish mass. Jake barreled into the room. He went straight to the second bed and sat on the trifold coverlet. The mattress wheezed.

"Jake?"

"I want a Coke."

"A Coke?"

"Do you have money for the machine?"

"Um. Yes." She scrambled for her purse.

"I hit him."

"What?" Bridget tried to yank her purse from the coat hanger, but it resisted. "Who?"

"Dad."

She kept fighting the coat hanger. "What?"

"I mean, push. I guess I pushed him."

She steadied her hand to find her wallet in her purse. She brought her wallet over to Jake.

"He was saying things about you, what you did. Things that weren't true."

She handed him a couple quarters from her wallet, the only quarters she had. In time, she'd learn to keep quarters and crisp ones on her, would learn that motel life would mean needing to have easy currency on your person and at the ready.

"Thank you," he said, taking the quarters. His palms were cold and damp.

Soon enough, they'd both become experts on motel life.

● **REC**

A light flares. The focus pulses before settling on the impossible whiteness of a bathroom. A toilet, a jar of potpourri on the tank. Someone just out of frame begins urinating forcefully. The sound alternates from the hiss of his stream hitting porcelain and tile to the small roar of incidental contact with the water in the bowl.

6.

A year later, Bridget and Jake weren't in a La Quinta Inn. They'd quickly run through the class of motels that could afford to sound like hotels. From there they downgraded to the tier of motels that punned off of sleep, like The Sleep Inn. But even those were too pricey to maintain residency at for long. Now, they were at the bottom tier, the motels that had numbers in the name, but not Super 8 or Motel 6; they aimed exclusively for the knock-offs, the ones with signs that were just big 7s glowing off the interstate.

They'd learned how to make it work. They'd learned to survive in places that did not always provide the basic necessities of hygiene. They'd learned to pilfer rolls of toilet paper wherever they could, often from the bathrooms of big box stores. They'd learned to bring their own toaster oven with them, that it was the most flexible of cooking appliances, that everything else were just scions of the toaster oven, their evolutionary developments making them more niche in application but less adaptable. They'd learned not to waste their time or money with motel laundry rooms, which were terrariums of mildew that gobbled quarters and returned your clothes with someone else's hair gnarled in the pockets. Instead, they sink-washed and hang-dried everything, a long process that meant there was never a single moment of a stay in which their living space was not flagged with damp shirts. This meant that part of their check-in ritual was to flip the doorknob tag to *do not disturb*. This meant that blasting the heater was a must, to expedite the drying process, even when it was already eighty degrees outside. It was in those moments when Bridget would pass by the hanging clothes and let their cool damp weight brush her face.

But it was not now eighty degrees. With winter starting to dull the crispness of autumn, the heater was welcome and by the time they were done hand-washing this load, their fingers felt numb, the hot water having run out halfway through. Bridget took a moment to hold her hands above the heating and air-conditioning unit beneath the window, let the warm attic-smelling air pass through her fingers, and when she turned back around she saw Jake on his bed with the Vernum catalog.

"Don't crease that," she said. "Only have six more."

"Aeronautics," he said.

She picked up the Trapper Keeper from the nightstand. "I'm gonna go find a fax."

"How do people believe this shit?"

She paused by the Marvin the Martian T-shirt hanging on a line strung between the bathroom door and the TV. She knew that such questions were not productive, that once she and Jake allowed room for incredulity, they gave up all hope of their marks believing. "They believe it because it's real."

"I mean, no high school I've ever heard of offers an aeronautics class."

"Well, it's not for you, Jake." She shoved the remaining quadrant of a Pop Tart into her mouth, its strawberry jam the closest thing to fresh produce she'd had in weeks. "You know when you got angry at the subtitles in that movie last week? You're not always the audience for everything."

"But this is a real class, right?"

"Aeronautics? Yeah, I mean, if that's what it says."

"You never read through this?"

"I did," she said. When she'd copied its contents at a computer in a Greeley Kinko's last March, she'd read through it primarily to make sure no reference to the original school went unedited. Aside from changing the school name, its mission statement, and contact information, though, it remained largely the same.

"And you think the real place actually offers an aeronautics class, or is that a lie too?"

"Not everyone is lying."

"I never got an aeronautics class." He tossed the catalog on the bed, then stretched his legs out. His foot nearly landed on the catalog. Bridget grabbed it, made sure it still looked new.

"You chose not to," she said.

"That's not true. No one ever offered me an aeronautics class."

"You chose to take the GED."

He held out his hand, aggressively waving it. "Give it back."

She handed him the catalog. "Be careful."

"What about these pictures?" He opened to a page that featured a full-page collage of students happily poring over books, staring thoughtfully into the ether. "Those are fake, right?"

Bridget sat on the foot of the bed, clutching the Trapper Keeper to her chest. "Those are stock photos. Models."

He looked over the pictures, his hands gentler with the pages now. "I'll tell Caleb that I go here. It'll make it believable."

"Well," she said, patting his socked foot. "I think I need to do his audition tape solo, but." She nearly cut her palm on Jake's toenails peeking through the holes in his socks. "Hun, we need to get you some new socks. Or at least a nail clipper."

"He'll ask what classes I'm taking." He flipped through the catalog with a rabbinical attention to the text. "Cultural Anthropology. Film and Literature. The History of Infinity?"

"That's math."

"Shit."

"Language, Jake."

"Oh, yeah. Says they require four years of language. I wouldn't do French again. I'd take Russian. D'you see they offer four levels of Russian?"

"Yeah." She stood up, re-velcroed the Trapper Keeper, slid on her tennis shoes. "You know why that is?"

"Because it's rad?"

"Because schools like that cater to the children of Russian oligarchs who don't want to raise their kids themselves and hope that an education at a private U.S. high school will launder both their reputation and their finances. Those are the kind of kids who go to whatever school I stole that from, and you, no matter what choices *you* make, will never be that."

"Nyet!" He raised his fist.

"It's not real, Jake."

"You said it *is* real."

"If it's not for you, it's not real. That's what 'not real' means."

"From the Latin."

"Probably."

"They offer Latin here, too."

"Good for them. And you know what? You're not taking it. Because you're here. Besides, why do you want to go back to high school? You passed the GED."

"I'm emancipated."

"Almost. A judge still has to say it."

"Emancipated," he said, his voice affected, as if imagining a judge pronouncing it.

"You know," she said. "I was emancipated when I was your age."

"If I took Latin, I'd go around talking Latin all the time and people would freak out. I'd be like an old knight and they'd think I'd time-traveled here. I'd be like, 'Suckus ma cockus.'"

"Jake, I'm your mother. I'm not the audience for those jokes."

"Well, you're the only person I know. Besides, we're peers now. I'm practically emancipated. Like the slaves."

"A little different."

"Maybe I'd know if I'd actually taken a fucking history class."

"Jake, language."

"They offer Chinese, too."

"Jake," she said, reaching for the catalog. "It's not real." She tried to take the catalog from him, but he held on to it. She pulled it away, tearing out one page. "Fuck."

When they'd finally found their car in the parking lot of the Foothill Square Mall, Jake had asked her when she was going to get a new car, as if the steps that dotted the timeline of every other life were still theirs to follow. She told him he'd bury her in this car, and the entire drive back to the Motel 7—or was it the 7 Motel?—he waxed logistically about how that could work.

Picking up the remote, he said, "I should go back to school. That's the real long con."

"You don't want to do that," she said. "School made you miserable. You remember Ms. Rombauer?"

"She played her oboe for us in class."

"Jake, she called you stupid."

"No, she didn't. She said I could get reading help. What's wrong with help?"

"Well, that's not how I remember it."

"I know."

"You don't need to go back to school."

"I never passed my genealogy project."

"Freshman year?"

He nodded.

"Why?"

"They said the information I provided wasn't reliable."

"They said I'm not a reliable source?"

"You seemed to really like telling me those stories. I didn't want to upset you by saying it was obviously untrue."

She said, "The part about the weaver was true."

"The one with the guts in her loom?"

"The warp and the weft, all that."

"What's that?"

"Warp and weft? That's—you know, fabric, some threads go up-down, others go side-to-side, each linking in the other."

"What's the difference?"

"The warp stays put."

"That seems backwards." Jake leaned back on the bed. "What'd they do with her again? The Weaver Witch."

"She wasn't a witch."

"But they must have burned her like one. Isn't that what happened to them?"

"Maybe if you'd taken a history class," she said, grabbing the Trapper Keeper.

"Har-har," he said, picking up the remote.

"You liked Ms. Rombauer? You didn't like Ms. Rombauer."

"She played her oboe for us."

"She was vile."

Bridget took the Trapper Keeper to the front office. The office was clearly, though mysteriously, a former room; it had the same layout as hers, but the bed had been replaced by a reception area, the landscape oil paintings on the walls replaced by OSHA notices. The windows had a view of the interstate.

The man behind the counter had a chinstrap beard which gave his face the architectural shape his chin no longer provided. His toque supported a hockey team on the other side of the country. People in these parts didn't have regional fandoms, just aspirational ones.

Behind him, on the counter, there was a small TV-VCR combo playing footage of baby sea turtles making their floppy ways to the ocean. David Attenborough was quietly narrating the probability of raptors swooping down and making a snack of these little gummies. They did look edible, their shells not even ossified.

When she asked the guy where she could find a Kinko's, he scrunched his brow and said, "Try 1993. They used to have one by Royal Tire but it got closed down. Used to be, people used it for making zines and band flyers for shows at the Garage, but all that stopped when Assemblies of God said it was a house of Satan, so no more band flyers. Pretty soon the only use people had for the Kinko's was photocopying their ass and they even cracked down on that. No pun intended."

"Gotcha." This man was clearly excited to have someone to talk to.

"You got a zine?" Behind him, the sea turtles had made it safely into the water.

"I actually just need a fax machine."

"Oh!" He clapped his hands. "We got one!" He presented to her the stout gray machine. It had been sitting there beside the TV the whole time. "A Hewlett-Packard."

"That's great!" She was happy to affirm his brand fetishism, and tolerating whatever psychotic small talk that passed as local color would be a small price for avoiding the Claymont Kinko's and its attendant risks. "I'll just be a minute," she said, starting to move around the counter.

He held up one meaty paw. "'Fraid I can't let you operate the Hewlett-Packard," he said. "I'd get written up for that. But I can fax your pages myself."

She looked at the pages in her hand, the scene of Anakin and Obi-Wan negotiating each others' ambitions with increasing suspicion. Faxing these pages to the Docters' house was already a risk. The number could be traced back to this motel where she'd registered with her real name. She'd need him to block the number, something they'd do at Kinko's where they were incurious about the tax returns and ransom notes they sent around the world. But this guy did not seem to have developed any professional incuriosity.

"Can you—" She couldn't think of a way to cover for this request, to make it anything other than what it was: suspicious. "Can you block the number?"

His eyes twinkled with prurient glee. "I know how to do that."

"Thank you." She handed him the pages, then Caleb's contact card. She pointed to the fax number he'd written down. "There, please."

He took the pages and moseyed over to the Hewlett-Packard. Turned three-quarters from her, hovering over the fax machine, he began reading.

"Not that many pages," she said. "Shouldn't take too long."

"Hmm." He flipped a page.

She could feel panic rising in her chest like something trying to escape. She put her hand on her sternum, pressed firmly.

"So you in the movies?" he said.

"I'm a—" She drummed a pen on the counter. "Casting

director." Then, suddenly nervous that he'd try to start angling for a role from her, she added: "For mostly younger performers."

"I see." He started typing in the Docters' number. After each beep, he gave a little "uh-huh."

Through the window, between the motel and the interstate, a small building sat abandoned. Opaque tarps covered the windows and billowed with the wind.

"How young?"

"Excuse me?"

"Younger performers, you said. How young?"

She watched a page slowly descend into the machine, the calming hum. "Well, that's for a teenager. Fifteen, sixteen."

"I see." He picked up the page after it had been fed completely through the fax machine; he seemed to be noting its warmth. "You know the Ramseys?"

"Um. Pharaohs?"

"Over in Boulder. JonBenét? Found dead last Christmas."

That abandoned building across the way, it had a sign out front, but she couldn't make out the lettering. "Yes," she said. "I read."

"Little girl. Performer." He fed another page into the machine. "Still no charges filed, no arrests."

"Do you like hockey?" She pointed to his toque. "My son played a bit. But he never learned to skate."

"So is it like a commission situation? Like if you find a good actor for a part, you get ten percent or something?"

"Not really," she said, pushing the nib of the countertop pen into the pad of her thumb.

"I've been doing some research," he said. "You know, if the Boulder police can't do anything, then it's all up to us, right?"

"Is that the last page?"

They trained her to be a little star," he said. "All that really means is she learned to follow orders."

"I must be going."

"Asphyxia by strangulation. Craniocerebral trauma."

The last page emerged from the bottom of the fax machine, and he put it on the thin stack. He brought the script back over to her.

"You blocked the number?" she asked, just enough breath in her lungs to complete the sentence.

"You should understand what they did to her. It's a real horror."

She took the script. "I don't think I should."

"It's all in my zine."

"Thank you," she said, making her way to the door.

The early evening air was cold on her face, felt calming. She could feel it in her lungs, a relief to know that air was getting in there.

She didn't want to go back to the room, not yet. She needed silence, genuine silence. Not the silence of Jake refusing to speak, but actual silence.

Clutching her tote bag, she ran across the parking lot, toward the abandoned building. Approaching the wind-blasted sign, she saw it was an old needle clinic.

The windows weren't just replaced by opaque tarps; they had been knocked out, though by intent or wind, she couldn't tell. Down here, away from the motel, the wind was hard, lashing her face.

Above, the blue sky was going gauzy with overcast. Not the kind that promised rain; the kind that just blanketed these ambiguous territories at this time of day, when dusk needed some assistance.

She pushed the tarp from the front door of the abandoned needle clinic like it was a shower curtain and went inside. There was a rain-damp couch in the corner. She sat down, breathed. The couch felt like sitting on an old sponge. She felt something sharp in her hand, saw a bead of blood forming in the webbing between thumb and forefinger. Little diamond-splinters of glass were all over.

Across from the couch was the counter, where, presumably, back when this place was operable, you'd check in for the needle swap, other what-have-yous. The counter was still filthy with flyers, sundry cures. Lots of God solutions, but, her eyes scanning over the more sciency brochures on display, she figured there was a God guy involved in those too somehow. On the front of the counter, someone had slapped a bumper sticker, fissured at the edges where fingers had failed to peel it loose. *There is no Chemical Cure for a Spiritual Problem*, it claimed.

The biggest regret of her mom's life was forgetting to bring film that day, the day she stood five feet from the man Zapruder. Bridget imagined her mother's fingers fumbling with the camera, her nails painted hammer-thwacked purple, though she now realized her mom never would have been wearing fingernail polish in 1963. Regardless, Bridget's mom didn't have the appropriate materials to capture that day's events—three firecracker punctures in the afternoon, a head coming apart like a watermelon, and the man Zapruder getting the shot, and the money. "The money," Bridget's mom said years later, "millions. That man Zapruder got all that, for pointing a camera."

By now, back home, maybe Mabel had found Bridget's parents.

When Jake, just a week after his sixteenth birthday, passed the GED, she'd been proud, sure, but she also recognized the acrid taste of shock and even disappointment. They'd celebrated with pizza, the whole time Bridget mourning the study sessions they'd shared in the months leading up to the exam: those evenings going through prep books, drilling him on formulae and dates, those evenings that felt like they were really building toward something—but building toward what, they'd never discussed.

By now, Caleb was surely reading over the script.

Her stomach was scraping itself out. She needed a real meal. She should get back to the motel, get out of this place. But its wreckage was oddly comforting,

Those medieval hicks who'd driven her weaver ancestor out of town, they could only see the wreckage of human gut on the loom, not the efforts of someone trying to salvage a situation, make something out of it. But who knew what the real story was. And who knew how her father—because he had been the one to pass on the tale of the weaver—had come into possession of that story.

Her relationship with her father had not ended when she won the court case against her parents, not entirely. She had seen him since then. Once.

The summer between her sophomore and junior years of college, she visited LA for the first time since leaving. She'd made the decision reluctantly, as if she'd pressured herself into it. For two years, she'd been telling people she was from LA, offering them a version of her life that she thought of as the closed version, the version that would not spark questions. In college, she wanted nothing more than to just be someone in college, and not be seen as an actress—or worse, a former child actress—taking her grand tour of bourgeois university life, just as Jodie Foster had gone off to Yale. (Indeed, to be a former actress attending a college that was not Yale was proof only of something deeply, suspiciously, wrong with her.) But—she couldn't avoid telling people that she'd come from Southern California. That was nicely vague, as she'd noticed that those who said they were from Southern California were usually from places like Bakersfield or Oxnard, hoping to be taken as a legit Angeleno, and this was her chance to use that geographic obfuscation to her advantage. Those curious enough to wonder what "Southern California" referred to exactly would assume she couldn't possibly mean LA. Still, every school break, people asked her if she was headed back to California. After a few breaks constructing reasons to stick around Boulder, or to take a seasonal job in Aspen, she finally folded—not, she realized, to the pressures of others, but to prove to herself that she had something to go back to. Even if she no longer spoke to her parents, she still had friends in LA. She must. And so, over the summer break between her sophomore and junior years, she decided to return to LA. After booking her flight, she called Ellie, who had changed her number, and she called Irina, whose answering machine clicked on after one ring. Both Ellie and Irina had been other young actresses who'd sued their parents for control of their finances; they'd all been introduced by their common attorney, and Bridget and Ellie had briefly been roommates. Bridget finally got through to Layla who seemed so happy to hear from her, Layla who Bridget had hired to help her write her college application essay, Layla who was now making sure she had Bridget's dates exactly right, saying, "Perfect, you can stay here." Bridget was taken aback, simultaneously heartened and frightened by Layla's hospitality. "Oh, that'd be so nice," Bridget said, and then Layla breathlessly explained that she'd be out of town and so Bridget would housesit and water her robust collection of ferns, lilies, and hydrangeas; a *parliament* of foliage is how she put it. Bridget wrapped the phone cord around her finger. "Lovely," she said. "They are lovely," Layla said, "and they're on a strict schedule. I'll print it out for you. I won't charge you for the stay." The trip back to LA, then, was mostly sitting in Layla's West Los Angeles apartment, a one-bedroom with a balcony facing the 405, a sticky note on the sliding glass door asking her to Windex it periodically because the exhaust from the freeway "mucked up everything." Bridget had nowhere in particular to go; her only obligation was to Layla's aggressively green leafware. For about a day, she thought she might find some interest in piecing together the details of Layla's life from the clues in her apartment. This detective work, though, proved fruitless, not for the lack of clues but for the lack of anything interesting that those clues revealed. The life that shed these clues—this assortment of VHS movies, this expired mayonnaise, these spare picture frames in the closet—were so lacking in any cohesive personality that they might as well have been curated by a set decorator with only the dimmest sense of character development. The potted plants were the only hint of a guiding passion in Layla's life. And screw those needy things.

She was pouring her Diet Coke into the soil of a potted something on the balcony when she heard someone say, "Ahoy, there!" This voice was coming from a man standing on the neighboring balcony. He was wearing a pink shirt that on second glance turned out not to be a shirt but rather his bare sunburnt chest. He introduced himself as Bob and began monologuing about all the nuances of his life that were already plainly obvious: that he was Layla's neighbor, that he'd suffered a bit of a sunburn, that he was not currently wearing a shirt. In exchange for such intimacy he asked for reciprocity: Who was she? Well, she was Bridget, and she was not sunburned, and she was wearing a Gap T-shirt. "Bridget," Bob said, turning to quaff the afternoon air, aswirl with the fumes of the 405. "Gaelic for 'little bridge,' if I'm not mistaken." He was mistaken, but she knew Bob wasn't interested in such trivialities, nor was he interested in letting her isolate in peace. No, the fellowship she'd come back to LA to find had, against her wishes, found her. Bob was a cunning interlocutor, though. In a matter of minutes, he'd extracted from Bridget—who offered these details as if in a demented but neighborly game of strip poker—how she knew Layla and that her secondary education had been primarily facilitated by people like Layla, having spent her adolescence not in high school but on the set of a terrible TV show. "An actress," Bob said, clapping his hands, not together but against his own torso, then wincing at the pain. "Lovely. Then I have your plans for the evening."

It was Bob, then, who inadvertently arranged the reunion of Bridget and her father.

Walking back to the motel now, she passed through a surprisingly full parking lot. As expert as she'd become at motel life, she'd never really come to understand her own demographic. She had no clue who were in these other rooms, their shades always drawn. She assumed the worst—deviants, snuff film auteurs, and weekend warriors on a final binge—as she knew they assumed the worst of her. She welcomed those assumptions. On those trips down to the car to bring up a bag, when a neighbor's gaze fell on her from a window, she embodied the role their fears cast her in. This act protected her. Not everyone's fears, though. She walked the long way around the motel to avoid passing the office again.

Walking up the stairs to her and Jake's room, she decided she'd get takeout tonight, somewhere with fresh produce. There was no Seasonality around here, but surely she could get a salad that wasn't just ranch-soggy iceberg lettuce and baby carrots the texture of her elbow. She suddenly wanted to crunch something green and stalky.

She opened the door, and the door met a sudden, clanging resistance. The door chain had been locked—Jake had locked it.

● **REC**

The image still has the glare of the bathroom, but is now streaked with something darker. A single corner of the frame is in focus: the helix loops of terrycloth in extreme closeup. The acoustics of this space finally allow for audible voices, two of them, one saying they should leave the camera here, running, the other saying that's how Chuck Berry got into trouble. A huff and the frame rattles. The light disappears as the audio blows out.

7.

Bridget pushed the door again. The resistance the chain offered was absolute, devastating.

"Jake? Honey?"

The frustration, the impotence, that the chain lock left you with was so total that her impulse was to just scream at the door. But instead she returned to the tone she took when Jake locked himself in the bathroom years ago for his masturbation jags.

"Everything okay?"

She put her ear to the four-inch opening the door offered. She only heard Jake mumble, "Wait, wait," followed by the sound of him fumbling around.

"Honey?" She tried to speak just loud enough for him to hear her while being just quiet enough to not cause any curtains in other rooms to part.

"I said wait!" The door slammed shut, knocking Bridget square on the forehead.

"Ah—damn it!" She rubbed her head furiously. She stepped back, eyes closed, until her heels hit the railing. She sat down and leaned back, resting her elbows on her knees, her head in her hands.

She opened her eyes, a headache dilating in her frontal lobe. Their room door appeared to be metal, the *do not disturb* tag hanging from the doorknob. If she'd ponied up for a room at a La Quinta, they might have had a wooden door, or at least something less concussive. She wondered if she was dizzy from brain bleeding or just plain hunger.

"Why you gotta be such an asshole?" she said.

"They're made that way." Above Bridget, a woman stood in a bathrobe. At one point, it had surely been fluffy and red, but its matted terry was now approaching shades of maroon like oxidized blood. "Men are just like that. Has something to do with how the lions need to defend their territory in Africa. Even after they're walking upright in America, they still got the old brain." She was holding a beige bucket. "I don't know about your room, but in mine the Nature channel is the only one that comes in clear, so."

"Old brain, huh."

"You want some ice? For your noggin?"

Bridget nodded.

The woman sat down beside her, the bucket sloshing with icy water. The woman pulled one trapezoid of ice from the bucket. Bridget reached for it, but the woman applied it directly to Bridget's forehead.

"That feel good?"

"It's—cold."

"Good." The woman's robe smelled so densely of cigarettes, Bridget felt like she was back in her childhood home. "If you need to stay in my room tonight, you can. I got the two beds."

Bridget recoiled, but the woman kept the ice on her. "What? Why?"

"The rooms just come with two beds. It's how it is."

"I mean, why would I stay there?"

"Listen, when my guy gets rough, it usually just takes till the morning till he's straight again. Could be that if he," she said, nodding at Bridget and Jake's door, "if he locked that door, it's for a reason you might want to respect. That's why I got my room, and that's why you can share it if you want."

"That's not—" Bridget stopped herself. The ice on her head was actually starting to hurt. She gently moved the woman's hand away. "It's—" She stopped again. She had no end to that sentence.

"It's all okay," the woman said. "Things get complicated. That's why I always have my club with me."

She kicked a steering wheel lock by her foot, its metal shaft coated in safety-yellow rubber with *THE CLUB* decaled across.

"You just carry that with you wherever you go?"

"In case things get complicated."

"What about your car?"

"Cars ain't complicated. People are."

On the other side of the door, Jake was fumbling with the chain lock.

The woman in the robe set down the ice bucket and reached for The Club.

Bridget touched her arm and she stopped.

The sound of the chain stopped. The door was surely unlocked now, but Jake wasn't opening the door.

Bridget turned to the Club-wielding woman. "Thank you." She stood up, wiped the ice water from her numb forehead, and stood at the door. She tapped lightly.

"Honey?" She heard only the wheeze of cars passing on the interstate. "I'm coming in, okay?" She turned the doorknob, was relieved when the door opened past four inches. As she entered the dim room and turned to close the door, she saw the woman in the robe clutching The Club.

The room was lit by the aquarium glow of the TV. Jake was on his bed, supine, staring comatosely at the screen. His chest betrayed the rapid breath he was trying to calm.

She put the Trapper Keeper on her bed. On the screen was the TV Guide channel, that sedating scroll of options, which was itself, more often than not, the preferred option. Jake could watch that scroll for hours.

"*Last Action Hero*," she said. "Channel forty-two. You like that one."

"No, I don't."

"Why—" She sat down on her bed. She stood back up. She went to the little desk in front of the mirror and picked up her new tweezers. "Why don't we get some nice takeout tonight? Like, something really nice?"

He flipped the remote in the air and caught it without looking.

She turned to the mirror, positioned the tweezer arms on either side of a single hair that had wandered astray, then closed in on it, plucked.

The tiny jolt of pain still ringing in her head—its precision a nice antidote to the dull ache of her gnawing headache—she said, "Were you talking to someone?"

He sighed. "I just locked the door because you said we had to be safe."

"*Point Blank*," she said. "Channel eight. You like that one."

"No, I don't."

"Were you talking to someone?"

"It was the TV."

She watched the scroll, listened to its saxophony Muzak, gooey with reverb.

She turned back to the mirror, couldn't find an errant hair so hastily plucked one—or three or four in a cluster—from the middle of her left eyebrow, felt the rush of pain.

She sat at the foot of his bed, blocking his view of the TV. He stared past her, through her.

"Apologize to me," she said.

He flipped the remote and, again, caught it without looking. He actually had some gross motor skills that a more observant parent could have leveraged toward something productive by now.

"You slammed the door in my face. You hurt me. Apologize to me."

"It's *Point Break* that I like. Not *Point Blank*."

He flipped the remote again and she reached for it, tried to snatch it out of midair, but instead she wound up swatting it away, and the plastic thing smashed against the headboard, batteries bursting out.

"Jesus Christ," he said, cowering.

At least it got a reaction from him.

As he searched the starchy bedsheets for a double-A, Bridget took deep, measured breaths and pulled the yellow pages from the floor. She hefted the floppy tome onto her lap and began thumbing through it for a place that might serve a fresh vegetable.

Jake, after fitting the batteries back into the remote, pointed it at the TV, his aim suddenly unsteady. The TV didn't seem to be responding. He said, "We need to go back to the P.O. box. I need to."

"The Farmer's Fork," Bridget read. "We'll try that?"

"I'll be quick. I'll take the car in a few days."

"Or Harvest Bowl," she read. "You know, I almost had to call the office for the battering ram."

"I was being safe," he said. He smacked the remote, aimed it again. "Why did you break the remote?"

"I think Harvest Bowl sounds the best," she said. "I'm ignoring your question."

"Obviously you're not."

“Why do you need to go to the P.O. box?”

He got up off the bed, like a man miraculously walking for the first time, and went to the TV. The TV was still on, still scrolling through the programing options. He just turned up the Muzak. “You use a battering ram on these doors and they’d make you pay like a thousand dollars to replace the door.”

“Honey, the P.O. box is strictly business. It’s not for some mailaway garbage.”

He stood in front of the TV, staring point blank—or maybe point break—at the screen. “I can use it, too. I’m allowed.”

“It’s not safe.”

“They have a hamburger?”

“What? You’re getting a hamburger mailed to our P.O. box?”

“The Farmer’s Fuck, or whatever. The Harvest Bowel. Do they serve hamburgers?”

Bridget looked at the two-square-inch advertisement in the yellow pages. It featured a contour-line cornucopia. “Probably.”

“Well done. No onions.”

“Who were you talking to?”

“I was being safe. I locked the door to be safe.”

“Real safe when you gave me a concussion.”

“You were smashing your face against the door. Who does that?”

“Apologize to me.” She stood up, gripping the yellow pages. “Goddamnit, apologize to me. You hurt me. Jake, you caused me harm. Apologize.” She felt a sting in her sinuses, a panicked shallowness in her breath.

He suddenly seemed scared of her, his eyes assessing a potential threat. “Can I just have a hamburger?”

She sat down at the little desk. She placed the yellow pages before her. She stared at the cornucopia, studied the unsure lines of apples and grapes overflowing. She knew she was crying. The blurring of her vision, the squish of her tear ducts. She watched herself as she watched the yellow pages.

"I'll do it," Jake said, and he reached for the wireless phone in front of her.

"No." She grabbed the phone. She heard him shuffle back to the bed.

The wireless receiver had a little digital display above the number pad. She held the receiver in both hands, steadied her thumbs above the numbers, looked from the Harvest Bowl's advertisement to the phone.

The left side of the digital display read, in segmented letters, *recent*. She could hear her breathing through now-congested nostrils. She clicked the little left-pointing arrow and saw the scroll of recent calls. Right there, at the top of the list, was the ten digits of their Denver home.

When someone at Harvest Bowl answered the phone, she figured she must have dialed. She ordered Jake's hamburger, well done, no onions. She ordered a large chef's salad. The woman on the phone said forty-five minutes.

She returned to her bed. They watched the TV Guide channel scroll through the better part of forty-five minutes.

NBC: *The Jeff Foxworthy Show*.

ABC: *Roseanne*.

CBS: *The Nanny*.

Fox: *Melrose Place*.

UPN: *Moesha*.

WB: *7th Heaven*.

By the time the NBC listing switched from *The Jeff Foxworthy Show* to *NewsRadio*, it was time to get the food.

Jake said he would get it.

He rooted through Bridget's purse and found her keys.

When he opened the door to leave, he said, "Jesus."

From outside came the voice of the woman in the robe: "Everything all good in there, sweetie?"

Bridget scrambled off the bed, went around the corner to see her son standing with his hands up in the doorway, the woman just outside holding up her Club.

"Yes, thanks," Bridget said. "We're all straight now."

The woman lowered The Club. Jake kept his hands up.

"I'm just in 217 in case things get complicated again."

Once the woman disappeared, back to 217 presumably, Jake left, closed the door without looking back.

Bridget returned to her bed.

TBS: *Dangerous Minds.*

TNT: *The Taking of Pelham One Two Three.*

There was something calming about this channel, the way is presented time as simple cobalt rectangles floating up and away. Time as a particle, something you could stack, sort, rearrange. In college, she'd taken a course in which the professor said that from a fourth-dimensional viewpoint, your life looked like a worm. And if you cut a worm in half, she'd thought, the head will regenerate a new body. But from a TV Guide channel viewpoint, your life looked like blocks neatly arranged. Characters, conflicts, and resolutions, all slotted in and contained.

USA: *Wings.*

Nickelodeon: *Dragnet.*

If Jake came back, she'd ask him about the call home.

ESPN: *SportsCenter.*

PBS: *The Civil War.*

She took a shower. The showerhead produced droplets that felt needly. It was a calcification problem. One day, she imagined, she'd stay somewhere long enough to invest her time into soaking one of these showerheads in lactic acid, to clear the calcium, the lime, the whatever. Invest her time. How many rectangular units of time would that be? She imagined handing them over, a physical, tangible currency she could press into the palm of someone. Of whom? Of someone who'd exchange it for what it was worth, who'd show her what it was worth, had been worth.

The soap, unwrapped from its little waxen envelope and pushed around her body with all the alacrity of that pumice stone (and where had she left that?), left her skin astringent. The towel still had the lushness of Velcro.

She got dressed in the same clothes.

Almost two decades ago, Layla's neighbor Bob had been a member of something called OvationNation. This was an organization he'd been part of for years, an organization with the mission of helping to find the extrovert in every introvert. What did that mean? Bridget asked Bob. It meant that public speaking was the single greatest fear across the entire human race, a fear greater than death, of terminal illness, of nuclear holocaust. That couldn't possibly be true. It was. According to what data? It was just true, Bob explained. He further explained that it was the goal of OvationNation to facilitate meaningful growth by helping people confront this fear greater than death. Bridget wondered if Bob had permanently replaced the term "public speaking" with "fear greater than death," and a fear that was greater than the fear greater than death dripped down the back of her neck: that this man was not going to stop talking.

By confronting this fear, Bob explained, people would go on to find fulfillment. Think, he implored her—or rather, he implored her to watch as he performed for her the act of thinking this thought, his arms outstretched, his gaze drifting toward the freeway—about all that could be accomplished when people were no longer held back by the fear greater than death. So how did this, um, organization—OvationNation, Bob reminded her—how did it accomplish such a feat of mass actualization? Simple, people give speeches. People get constructive feedback. People get certificates. They held quarterly speech contests, in which rising Ovationeers competed against each other—friendly competitions, of course—and the winner received the title of Master of Ceremonies. So it's not a cult, Bridge wanted to know. It was an NPO. Bridget had never heard that term before, but she nodded and she realized she was still nodding when Bob said their quarterly contest was tonight and that they needed a judge to fill in, after Alex had been arrested. "We would be honored to have a professional performer as one of our evening's arbiters." Bridget explained that she was no longer an actress, that she was a college student now. Bob wanted to know where. She said Yale. He did not seem to recognize the name, but he said again that she would be an ideal guest arbiter, that OvationNation provides a clear and easy-to-follow rubric, and that it would mean a great deal to the speakers. But she insisted that she wasn't an actress anymore, that she was just normal now. "No," Bob explained to her, "you are not normal." And she agreed to do it. She wasn't entirely sure why. As Bridget tended to Layla's terrarium, she told herself that she'd agreed just to get him off her back, but of course that didn't make sense and she knew it, and as she got ready for the evening she found herself taking extra care to appear not like the self she'd insisted upon—the college student in the Gap T-shirt—but like the self that she'd demurred from, an industry professional, someone whose métier was self-possession. She wore an Ann Taylor top.

The event was held at a church in Culver City. The church was either nondenominational or merely reticent in its convictions, the decor more the stuff of clearance bins than a strident theological aesthetic. As things were getting settled, as people were slowly filing in, this setting lent the event the ambiance of a twelve-step group, the coffee machine—the bitter bouquet of cheap grounds mixed with vinegar from a recent cleaning—percolating in the corner. She was greeted by multiple men with laminated name tags and a performative sense of social interaction. They shook her hand and motioned to the pulpit with the practiced gestures of people who'd only recently learned to use their arms. She found it oddly comforting, soothing. They were all very excited for her to be one of the evening's arbiters. They told her: "We're all very excited for you to be one of tonight's arbiters." They prompted her to sit on a folding chair in the apse, just behind the altar where the podium stood. There were three chairs and she sat on the one to the far left. Soon arrived the two other judges for the evening, a married couple, Mr. and Mrs. Dover. They moved one chair so they could sit on either side of her. This was ostensibly because of their hearing; they didn't want one person to have to strain to hear Bridget, but the effect of the rearrangement felt like they were surrounding her—and they *were*. They handed her photocopies of the grading criteria. Apparently they were supposed to keep track of how many times the speaker used placeholder sounds like *uh* and *um*, and even phrases like *you know* and extraneous *wells*. But not to worry, Mrs. Dover explained, she had plenty of experience being the *ah* counter at meetings, so she would take care of that part. And Mr. Dover assured her that she wouldn't have to worry about the eye-contact index, as that took years of experience to properly assess, knowing the difference between eye contact that was pro-social and eye contact that was anti-social. "That's more an art than a science, kind of a feeling—like, based on this eye contact, do I think this person will hug me or hurt me?" They both just assured her that all she had to worry about was getting a general feeling for the speaker, the texture of their character, and then they'd discuss. Mr. and Mrs. Dover were, though initially intimidating, quite comforting. They had a protective parental vibe.

As the event itself got going, Bob—standing uncomfortably in a Hawaiian shirt, exposed skin glistening with aloe—went over the rules for the attendees, then introduced Bridget as a professional actress there to be a guest judge. He introduced the three contestant speakers for the evening, all of them seated in the front pew. In the aisle seat, slated to go first, was her father.

Jake came back to the motel room. He placed her food on her bed, his food on his.

She opened the packet of dressing. It was a vinaigrette, more viscous than normal. She had difficulty evenly distributing it around the salad.

The TV Guide channel unspooled time in boxes that increasingly seemed unfilled, TBD.

She told herself that when *Dragnet* ticked over to *I Dream of Jeannie*, she'd speak.

They listened to the squish of each other eating.

Nickelodeon: *I Dream of Jeannie.*

"It's okay that you talk to your dad, you know." She said this with food in her mouth, hoped it could absorb, muffle, whatever he might hear in her voice.

Jake put a French fry in his mouth. "He just got some mail

for me, is all."

"What?"

"He just wants to send some of my mail."

"No, I mean: what mail?"

Jake shook his head. "Nothing. The GED."

"The diploma?" A cherry tomato fell from her mouth.

"Or whatever it is. A certificate maybe."

"That's great. We could frame it."

"I don't want to be here."

Bridget closed the clamshell box on her salad. "*Point Break*. Do you want to watch it?"

He pointed a fry at the TV. "It said *Point Blank*."

"I mean, pay-per-view. We could buy it. Splurge. It's available, just like that." She snapped her fingers. She had no idea if the movie was available.

Jake said, "No."

"Honey, I need you. I need you here. What would I do without you?"

"I know it's okay to talk to Dad. I don't need permission. We talk."

"We'll get it framed. I know where there's a place. I saw it from the freeway. We can pick out the frame. For the diploma."

"Certificate."

He looked at his feet and spoke with a well-rehearsed meter: "If this next one works out, it'll be my last."

"You just want a place to hang the frame, I get it. What's the point of framing something if you don't have a wall of your own to hang it on? I want that too. And we'll have it, soon. I promise. Just as soon as we're all settled up."

"Caleb said he has a sister. Could be a double deposit."

"What would I do without you?"

"Dad's not even angry anymore."

The naivete of that, the child offering consolation to the parent, told her how much she'd failed, failed to impress upon him the breadth and depth of the world's scorn. She wanted him to tell her, just once, that it was hopeless.

"How's your burger?" she asked.

"Still cold and raw in the middle."

● **REC**

Faces emerge into clarity only to be attacked by pixels in geometric paroxysms. This is the perspective of something briefly airborne, something spun, something now tucked under an arm, something now taking interest in black-clad people assuming their positions beneath black sheets draped over a wall. In a moment, they become extensions of the wall, the ambient pings of giggles suppressed.

8.

By the time Bridget and Jake left for the Docters' house two days later, the bruise in the center of Bridget's forehead glowed purple at the center, flared orange at the edges. A layer of make-up only turned the whole thing a jaundiced yellow.

The Docters' house was in a gated community tucked into foothills out beyond a cluster of new commercial developments. To gain ingress, Bridget had to give her name—Sarah—to a guard perched in what appeared to be a tollbooth. It felt like driving onto the studio backlot when she was a teenager.

Sitting now at the end of the cul-de-sac where the Docters' ersatz Victorian loomed like a gingerbread house frosted beige, Bridget turned off the Camry's engine. It cooled in the October air, pinging faintly.

The rest of the cul-de-sac featured houses that couldn't quite figure out what they wanted to be. Massive, they seemed assembled as if in architectural games of exquisite corpse: a miniature rotunda above porticoes with florid abaci, here a mansard window, there a ghoulish set of ocular windows. If the fortress-like design of the neighborhood wasn't enough to convince them, the slapdash chaos of these houses telegraphed the kind of wealth—the kind of wealth that caused architects to swallow their pride and follow money-green whims—that she and Jake were looking for in a mark.

Jake had been right. He'd been the one to spot Caleb, to approach him. And that's, ultimately, why he was here, sitting next to her in the Camry. He'd never gone along for this part, but he'd convinced her that he was the one Caleb trusted, not her, that she needed him as a kind of token of authenticity. They'd come up with his backstory: how she'd found him skating outside the Galleria in Los Angeles and convinced him to submit a tape for a Mountain Dew commercial, which he booked, and shortly thereafter she got him a reading with NBC for a pilot. And now, when he didn't have an acting gig, he worked as a casting assistant for Sarah.

"But you don't skate," she'd said. "Or can you?"

"I could skate," he'd said, "if you'd given me that board I wanted in sixth grade."

"You have bones as strong as a robin's egg," she'd said. "You think you'd do well falling off a skateboard?"

"In this version, I'm a skater."

And now, sitting in the Camry outside the Docters' finely crenellated house, she noticed he had the wrong shoes. Skaters wore the kind of shoes that were simple and striped, shaped as if suction-cupped onto their skateboards. But Jake's shoes, they were clearly the shoes of someone who'd never excelled at athletics, clearly the shoes of who Jake was, not who Jake was trying to be. They were all black, as if worn by a busboy who needed both ergonomic support and to satisfy a strict dress code. The backs were caved in a bit, the sign of someone shoving their feet into them like they were slippers.

"You sure you got this?" she asked him.

"Mom, stop."

Maybe the bad shoes were good. Maybe the bad shoes would somehow sabotage the whole thing. Maybe his condition for going home, successfully conning the Docters out of two deposits, would be the trip wire that kept him with her, kept him from going back to Tod. Tod, who'd let his son run off, run off with a criminal, run off with her. The life she'd given him this past year was a life in which he'd thrived, found ways of being, of being himself. This was a life not available to him back in Denver, that life of teachers telling him he wasn't focusing, of counselors euphemizing his challenges, challenges that didn't prevent him from passing the GED, challenges that proved inconsequential when compared to what she could do, how she was able to guide him to success on the GED, her son, a kid who'd basically graduated high school two years early by dint of not being in high school, by the grace of the life that she'd been able to provide him. And now he wanted to go back to Tod: Tod, who'd let his son run off, run off with a criminal, run off with—her.

It was that point, the point at which self-defense veered uncontrollably into self-indictment, where all thoughts led. It was inevitable, acute.

She needed the money in that house, and she needed this plan to offer some sort of trap door escape from what that money would buy her son.

She touched his hair.

"I shampooed," he said.

"I didn't say you didn't."

"Well, you kind of did. You're always checking."

She popped the trunk. "Can you get the camera?"

"Oh, no!" He pointed, stubbing his finger against the windshield. "Bike cop!"

Sure enough, a security guard for the neighborhood pedaled around the cul-de-sac. He seemed pretty young, and Bridget was relieved to see only a yellow stun gun on his belt, which looked more like a squirt gun than a real gun. He attempted a wheelie on his way out of the cul-de-sac, but his front wheel only got an inch or two off the ground.

"You seem pretty excited," Bridget said. "Is that like a slug-bug thing?"

"Mike Porter, he used to chase those guys around. It was so funny."

"That kid who was under house arrest?"

"He was so funny."

That's what Jake wanted to go back to, apparently. If he was going to be a criminal, it was her duty to at least offer him a more respectable model of one.

With him, she was a parent; without him, she was just a crook.

Standing outside the car, he got the Panasonic DV Pro from the trunk. The other houses had a light smattering of Halloween decorations, but nothing extravagant. Aside from the pumpkins, there were some plastic ghosts taped in windows and skeletons on doors. She would have expected more in a neighborhood like this. She would have thought a neighborhood like this to be some Wonka's chocolate factory of Halloween spectacle, for rich kids only. But no: these decorations evinced the same level of indifference that exhausted parents demonstrated everywhere.

Places like this were ninety-five percent white, five percent terrified.

The Docters' porch had only two pumpkins, rudimentarily carved with features that showed only basic geometric skill, nothing else. Was it that Halloween was just for the poor and middle class? Was it that once you got to this level of advantage, you simply had no use for rituals of the uncanny and the horrific? Maybe the rich—the truly rich, not the mere comfortable, as she and Tod had been—knew the control they exerted extended to all realms, including the bodily and the eschatological, so what use was zombie-inspired dread? Those rituals exorcised nothing for them, and so, when finally insulated from the cheap rubber masks of the hoi polloi, they let their indifference show with a couple dullard jack-o-lanterns.

Bridget rang the doorbell. It echoed dimly inside like a rumor.

A young woman opened the door. She was either a teenager striving for the affectations of adulthood or an adult aching for her youth. She wore a massive sweater in a way that telegraphed both comfort and contempt, and her eyes were winged with dark eyeliner. "Catering?"

"Casting," Bridget said.

Jake asked, "Is Caleb here?"

She shrugged. That was a dumb question. She walked back into the house, leaving the door wide open.

Jake looked at Bridget. She shrugged, then stepped over the threshold. She'd once been a person who needed explicit permission to do anything. As a kid, she'd ask to use the bathroom even when at home. An on-set acting coach told her that she needed to treat all spaces as if she already lived there, treat all people as if they already loved her. She didn't believe that any space was hers, or that anyone actually loved her, but she did believe in that acting advice.

The foyer was big enough to be an actual foyer, not just a transition space to drop grocery bags. It opened up into an option of living rooms not unlike those in Ethan's home over in Claymont: one clearly for use, one clearly for show. She picked the lived-in living room, as she was pretty sure that's where she saw the young woman whisk her sullen self off to.

There was a domino game of couches, loveseats, chaise longues. On the wall, a video projector was showing a movie. A

Halloween movie, possibly *Halloween*. Strewn about in the collision of furniture were boxes, opened and containing nothing but crisp white Styrofoam: the remains of a shopping spree.

"Hello." A voice, an older man. Bridget couldn't figure out where it was coming from, though. "Are you qualtagh?"

As much as she wanted to hold her space, she was disoriented, couldn't make out which way was which, or maybe the voice was coming from the surround sound of the projector TV. And where was Jake? Had he taken a wrong turn into the other living room?

"Are you qualtagh?" Finally, a person emerged as the owner of that voice. A man in a crisp pinstripe button-up, untucked over jeans that were more like denim slacks than anything Levi Strauss ever imagined. He was barefoot on white tile.

"Casting," Bridget said. "I'm Sarah."

"Of course, of course." The man briefly covered his face in mock embarrassment. "We spoke. I'm Roger Docter."

He was right. They had spoken, when she'd called to arrange Caleb's taping. He'd been busy, though, and seemed distracted. Now he was looking at her with a discomforting focus.

"Dr. Docter to the kids."

"Oh!" This came out like a hiccup, too sudden to stifle. "You're a real doctor?"

"I'm just glad my last name isn't Helot."

She smiled, wondering if she'd heard that right, wondering what that meant.

He said, "So you're my qualtagh."

"You said that."

"It means the first person you see after leaving your house in the morning—a predictor of what that day will bring."

"It's not morning."

"It's morning somewhere."

"But I'm *in* your house."

He looked around, eyed the pristine clutter of his living room. He raised his hands with priestly ease. "So you are."

"Is Caleb here?" She looked around, saw no sign of Jake.

"Qualtagh." He wandered over to a nearby couch, looked under a blanket. "From my word-of-the-day calendar." He moved to the chaise longue. "Caleb?" He picked up a throw pillow, as if his teenage son could hide beneath it, cozied up like a mouse.

Bridget, oddly comforted by the specter of someone as self-possessed as Dr. Docter having also misplaced his son, said, "What does that mean—like, what *about* that person? About the ... qual-tag?"

"Not sure. I mean, it's an omen, right? Maybe it was Gaelic? Kind of sounds Gaelic. Ever been there? Kiss the Blarney Stone?"

"Did Caleb get a chance to look over those scenes? I'm thinking this could be a great space to tape. The acoustics are nice. Ha." She paused, gesturing to the resonance of her bark in the arched ceilings. "Ha."

"In the Blarney Castle near Cork," he said. He bent down and picked up a flip-flop. "Caleb's around here somewhere." He tossed the flip-flop beneath a projected Jamie Lee Curtis being chased by a masked lunatic with a kitchen knife and a stiff back. "Big slab of limestone. People come from all over to pucker up to it. It's disgusting, and quite exciting."

"Did you have a chance to chat with Caleb about the scenes? It's a pretty great opportunity. You like *Star Wars*?"

"You ever done that?"

"Acted? Yes, I have."

"You ever put your mouth where countless others have?"

She bumped her shin on an end table. "I need to find my—associate. Have you seen him? Young man with a camera?"

Dr. Docter opened a cabinet, and instead of revealing a teenager inside, he pulled from a shelf a bottle of something brown. "So we're looking for two people now? This house just swallows people up. Donut?" He held up the bottle, an offer.

"That's not a donut."

He looked at the bottle, then at her. "You passed the fabled whiskey-or-donut test." He smiled, then pulled a tumbler from the shelf and poured himself a few fingers.

"Sorry, I just misheard."

"So, Ms. Herd, Ms. Casting Director, Ms. Qualtagh, my Gaelic omen, are you a good omen or a bad omen?"

He advanced on her as she retreated backward, toward what she imagined was the kitchen. Strange, she realized, with this barefooted man walking toward her, how the mind makes the layout of a house independent of experiential knowledge.

"I think I'm pretty good."

He pointed at her forehead. "You have a third eye."

She wasn't sure how much more of his mishmashed, misapprehended spiritual and folkloric scraps she could tolerate. But her job here wasn't just to tolerate him; it was to flatter him, to become essential to him and his visions of the future, a new future that she would have to help him imagine. She touched her forehead, if only to acknowledge his comment. She felt the putty-like texture of foundation and realized he'd been referring to the bruise in the center of her forehead. "It was—just an accident."

Dr. Docter nodded. "I see accidents like that a lot. Do you feel afraid to go home?"

"Oh," she said, turning away. "No. It's not—it's not that. It actually was just an accident."

"If you need a place to go," he said. His tone still had the flirtatious snark, which made her feel queasy. He left that sentence hanging and started a new one: "I'll bet he apologized."

"He did," she said.

He smirked. He'd won, his face said, proven that he'd been right about his suspicions. He now appeared deeply satisfied by the idea that she was married to an abuser. "Uh-huh. I'm sure he promises every single time that he'll never do it again. Right?"

"It wasn't like—" But she stopped herself. It wasn't her job to tell him he was wrong. It was her job to flatter him, to become essential to him. "Yes," she said.

"I'm always right about these things."

As she was trying to strategize about how to leverage whatever nascent hero complex this might activate in him, the focus of his eyes shifted to something else—her neck, maybe, or her ear. How many accidents and misconceptions were her body bearing proof of? But no, he was looking at something behind her. He stopped advancing. His smile changed, became less oblique, more ready for school picture day. "There we go."

Bridget turned, hoping to see Jake, hoping to see Caleb. Instead it was the young woman who'd opened the door. She leaned as if against a doorway, though her body was propped up only by her own obstinacy. To Dr. Docter, she said, "Did catering mention donuts?"

Dr. Docter said, "You already in costume, Chrissy?"

Bridget said to her, "I'm not catering. I'm a casting director. I'm looking for—"

"Then when's catering getting here?" Chrissy said.

Dr. Docter said, "That was a joke about your mascara, sweetie. The costume comment. Looks spooky, your makeup."

Chrissy turned and left. Bridget could see around the

corner now, saw the fluorescent glow that suggested she was right: The kitchen was over there.

"Disaffected by Maybelline," Dr. Docter said, sipping his drink.

That must have been the sister Jake had mentioned. The sister he thought they could get to read, put on tape, lure into dropping a deposit for a fake on-set high school. If that was going to work, Bridget would have to convince her that she, Bridget, was not the catering, that she was someone who had actual cache, had something worth wanting. Something other than a donut.

Bridget looked down at her clothes, could see how Chrissy would make that mistake. The black jeans and stretchy black top did have an air of the service industry, though to Bridget this look had always seemed professional, but of a particular profession: These were, to her, theater blacks. Breathable black clothes optimized for movement. This was the look of someone who'd been professionalized on a set, behind a stage. This was a uniform that communicated trustworthiness.

Peaty breath was now enshrouding her. "So what's this movie?"

"The prequels to *Star Wars*," she said, her hands at her chest as if ready to block an advance. She was, however, relieved to have a familiar script. "George Lucas is making movies about Darth Vader when he was young, like how he became—that."

"And Caleb wants to do that, huh?"

"I think," she said, nodding, smiling, trying to switch back into character: focusing on needs, desires, *the task*. "I think he could be really good. I'm not often wrong about these things. Did you see *My Girl*?"

Dr. Docter sipped, didn't answer.

"I cast the little girl in that, discovered her selling Girl Scout cookies."

He nodded. His eyes were focused on her face, but not her eyes. Bridget tried to move slightly to the left to align her eyes with his.

He said, "Think we have some old Tagalongs in the kitchen."

He walked past her. For a flashing moment, she thought he was going to walk right through her.

"And maybe a Caleb or two," he said, his voice fading down their hallway, echoey from all the tile.

Bridget's gaze darted around the room, as if Jake could have been hiding in here the whole time. Of course he wasn't. Of course she'd lost track of him. Of course he was already going off script.

Her father's speech that night at OvationNation's quarterly contest began as follows: "When I saw the theme for this evening's event—learning through embarrassment—it occurred to me that I could very well tell a story about giving my first speech at OvationNation. Indeed, the first time I addressed my fellow Ovationeers, I stumbled over my words so much, the *ah* counter lost track of how many superfluous words I'd used. I was so nervous, I was only able to string together *ums* and *huhs*. If I uttered one real word in that whole mess, I don't remember it. But that was some time ago now, and I've gone through a great deal of growth. I owe that growth to the lessons I learned not just from that moment of, yes, embarrassment, but from the community I have found here at OvationNation. So, thank you." He paused, accepting the light smattering of applause with a nod.

This was not her father. True, this man standing at the podium, this assemblage of cells and Old Spice, was her father, but the words he pulled together offered a man who was not the father she knew. The father she knew never would have stumbled over his words in front of others. The father she knew was perhaps only comfortable when hamming it up for others.

He continued: "For a while, I made my work as an extra in movies and television. I always thought it strange, being *extra.* Both apt and not. You're both superfluous and necessary. They also call you scenery. You're supposed to be seen but not *seen.* As a young man I enjoyed the work, as it simply required me to be entirely passive. They told me where to go, where to sit or stand, walk this way or that way, and I did it. They gave you free lunches in brown paper bags, entirely anonymous except for those marked vegetarian. I knew some extras who were vegetarian, and this always caused a bit of an issue when lunch came around, making sure they had the right lunch sack, and so I decided I would never be a vegetarian. I did not want to hassle anyone."

The father she knew loved nothing more than to hassle everyone, and when he'd worked as an extra, he side-hustled by gathering autographs from whichever celebrities happened to be on that day's call sheet, later selling the autographs to collectors.

"One day, I was in a crowd scene. A bunch of us, we were crowding a street, running away from a large monster that did not exist. The assistant director, a man with a bullhorn, told us all that we'd be running away from the monster that did not exist. To give us proper motivation to run from this monster, the man with the bullhorn described him as being very big and very vicious. Rather like a lizard but much, much bigger. One of my fellow superflu-actors." He paused to let the cleverness of his neologism bubble up a few laughs. "—asked if he meant Godzilla, and the man with the bullhorn yelled no, not anything like that and if anyone suggested that this film was about that character owned by Toho Company they would be escorted off the set without their day's sack lunch. So this not-Godzilla, we were told, was bearing down on us, and we simply had to run down this street. The camera, he said, would be filming in slow motion, which meant there would be no audio recorded, so he would continue to bark at us through the bullhorn while the camera was rolling."

Minutes earlier, as Bridget's father had approached the podium, he'd avoided looking at Bridget, with whom he now shared a stage. She was watching him from behind, from her view in the apse, and even though she could not see his face as he delivered this speech, years later she'd have a clear memory of his expression.

"When they started rolling, we were told to run. And I did. And I couldn't figure out why everyone was running faster than me. The man behind me was clearly annoyed at my pace. The man with the bullhorn yelled cut. He was standing on a platform constructed behind us, on which the camera was perched. Through his bullhorn, he directed us back to starting positions, and we obliged. He reminded us that a big scary lizard creature was right behind us, and we were running for our lives. We began a second take, and again I seemed to be the slowest one. Now the man with the bullhorn seemed quite agitated. To the entire crew and cast of extras, he said, 'You there, in the yellow shirt.' I looked down. I was wearing a yellow shirt. The man shouted, his voice amplified for hundreds of people, 'Why are you running in slow motion? Run normal! The camera does the slow motion!'"

The OvationNation audience laughed. Beside Bridget, Mr. and Mrs. Dover laughed.

"Yes," her father said, "that's exactly how all those hundreds of people responded, too. There I'd been, apparently running in some mock slo-mo, without realizing it. That was all the feedback I needed to snap out of it and begin to do as instructed, but all those people laughing like that—well, at first, I was simply embarrassed. I must have looked so foolish. But as this evening's theme suggests, embarrassment can instigate learning and growth. I realized that it had not just been about me misunderstanding the instructions. It had been about me imagining myself through the eyes of others. Prioritizing an external view rather than my internal experience. If I thought someone saw me in slow motion, then I lived in slow motion."

In the pause her father left before the final coda, Bridget caught a glimpse of the night's trophy for best speech. Her father had never had a fear of public speaking, but he did have a fear of not getting all the trophies. This trophy was an old condenser microphone, gold and big as a fist, perched atop a mahogany plinth.

"Now? Well, now I live my life at full speed."

The audience applauded. Beside Bridget, Mr. and Mrs. Dover applauded. Her father stepped to the side of the podium so he could bow unobstructed. Cupping his hands together, he said, "Thank you for listening to my story."

It was not, however, his story. It was Bridget's.

In Dr. Docter's living room, she paced between couch and loveseat to gather herself, remind herself of the plan.

Or at least what preceded a plan: a need. She needed to keep Jake.

On the shelf that held the turntable—oh, and there was a

turntable—sat a fat dictionary. It was old, the fabric of its spine worn thin like cheesecloth. She hefted it, sat down and let its comforting weight on her lap calm her, focus her. She opened the big book. It smelled like whatever estate sale the Docters had bought it from.

Above her, Jamie Lee Curtis was hiding in a closet.

Bridget flipped through the dictionary, the clothy resilience of the paper smooth on her fingers, until she found it: *Helot: /ˈhelət/. noun*. "Lower social class," she read. "Laborers kept in captivity," she read. "State-compelled breeding," she read. She closed the book, but kept it on her lap for a moment. She held the cover down, as if to keep something locked in there.

Jamie Lee Curtis was fighting back, stabbing. But she paused, her image flickering in stasis.

"I want music," someone said. Caleb said. His voice, in the room.

He was in the doorway, one of the doorways, holding a remote, having just announced that he wanted music as if to someone, though he clearly was not aware of the only other person in the room: Bridget, who was now struggling to get up, get the book back on the shelf, get Caleb's attention, Caleb who was already walking away, walking down the hall, back to the foyer.

"Caleb," she said, trying to follow him. "Yoo-hoo!"

When she got into the foyer, she found it filling from the open front door with a dozen people, all of them carrying plastic shopping bags overflowing with the crinkly stuff of Halloween fare, or large rolled-up tarps, or cardboard boxes, or pieces of lumber.

Caleb was already occupied with greeting these people, mostly his peers. He seemed to then be directing them to different parts of the house.

The boy holding a piece of plywood the size of a door said, "Gonna be a sick haunted house. Scuse me, ma'am."

As he squeezed by her, the splintery fresh-cut edge of the plywood pulled at the material of her shirt.

● **REC**

Sound blown out, the distortion moves in churns, something subaquatic about the swirl of sound, while the image regains focus: people moving plastic bodies, gripped underarm like surfboards. A young man directs them out of frame. The image jolts, rushes through space, suddenly has the mise-en-scene of a rinse cycle. Then something like time travel, a new space, quiet and still, a bedroom, the reassuring assortment of teenagery mess.

9.

Through the scattering crowd, Bridget managed to tap Caleb on the shoulder. The boy turned around. He was recently showered, his hair still damp and redolent of Head & Shoulders. He regarded her as if she were—

"Catering?"

"What? No." Bridget smoothed the front of her shirt, as if she could rub a new color into her theater blacks. "Caleb, it's me. Sarah. The casting director? Did you have a chance to read through those scenes?"

"Oh, yeah," he said, showing no shift from his earlier misapprehension of her.

"'Yeah,' as in, you took a look at them? Or 'yeah,' as in, you remember me?" She chuckled to deflate some of the anxiety she knew was audible in that last sentence.

"Yeah, yeah," he said, then turned to a girl holding a rubber corpse. "In the downstairs bathtub," he said, pointing.

"So we're going to tape your audition, right? Are you excited?" She gave him a light punch on the arm.

He considered his arm with curiosity.

"We'll need a quiet space," she said. "How about upstairs? Have you seen, um—" She blanked on Jake's character's name. "Have you seen my associate?"

"Yeah," he said, the word beginning to sound more like a verbal tic than an assertion of consent. Although, if it was an affirmative, then an affirmative to what? She'd asked two questions again. She needed to stop doing that, letting herself avalanche questions upon people. Was he ready to tape his audition or did he know where Jake was? Either way, she was following him, down the hall, past framed family photos: Caleb, Chrissy, and the good doctor, in matching turtlenecks, the kids just young enough to be compliant. No mother to be seen, as if she'd been meticulously edited out of the scene.

Caleb was now heading upstairs, the stairs carpeted, the carpet clean enough for Bridget to suddenly worry that this was a shoes-off house. A strange, irrational worry, considering the house was now being overrun by teenagers in Doc Martens, muddy prints left like cubist skulls. But awareness of the irrationality of this worry did not seem to short-circuit it. The thought—innocuous, but somehow insidious—followed her up the stairs, as she followed Caleb.

At the top of the stairs, Caleb turned. To Bridget, three steps below him, he said, "Oh."

He had not, apparently, intended for her to follow. Bridget the intruder, Bridget the interloper. Bridget—*treat all spaces as if you already lived there, treat all people as if they already loved you*—said, "Well, come on, let's get going." She continued up the stairs and pushed by him onto the landing. "Which way?" She turned her fingers out, one hand pointing in each direction like a road sign, then gave a flapping laugh. "We'll need a quiet room. Good acoustics, good lighting. Preferably just a plain white wall as a backdrop. Oh, and I'll need my associate. He has the camera. Are you off-book?"

He seemed off balance, or swaying in that palm-tree way of

lanky young men. "Oh, yeah," he said. "Well. I can do that, but in a minute."

"You read through the script, yes?" Upstairs, where there weren't any of his friends trouncing around, it was much quieter, but she was still speaking as if to be heard over the noise of teenagers.

"Sure. I mean, I'll do it. Of course. But—I'm kinda busy." He turned to walk away, and Bridget must have mirrored his movement because he instantly stopped, squared his body to hers as if to a strange and potentially dangerous animal.

She clenched her fists, immediately unclenched them, stifled a *sorry* and said, "Quite the party you're throwing here."

"Haunted house. It's a tradition."

"Kinda weird for you to invite us over to do the audition tape when you're throwing a haunted house, huh?" She bit the inside of her cheek.

"You spoke to my dad."

"Doctor Docter, right?"

"He doesn't know anything." He looked around, scrunched his face. "Listen—come here."

He waved for her to follow, but instead of heading down the hall, he went down the stairs. He took two, three steps at a time. She hurried to keep up with him, but worried she'd trip, fall down the stairs, collide into him, send him headfirst into the wall, bloody his face, spray his broken teeth like shrapnel—

At the bottom of the stairs, he turned down the hall, away from the familiar direction of the living room. She followed him into what turned out to be the laundry room, about the size of her and Jake's entire motel room. In one dark corner, a Nautilus weight machine had been abandoned, its levers and pulley systems like some medieval torture apparatus. Against the wall stood the washer and dryer, in one corner a large basin sink, and along the walls cabinets. On top of the front-loading dryer was a stack of—

"Whole chickens," he said. "Straight from the butcher."

There were about half a dozen of them, all wrapped in white paper, each bundle the size of her torso.

Caleb grabbed a plastic bucket from under the sink, placed it beside the dryer, and said, "I need you to gut 'em. Pull out the organs, bones, anything that seems, you know, *good*. Toss it all into that bucket."

She knotted her fingers together at her sternum. "You want me to help you get dinner ready?"

"Gonna use it for the dark room. You know, people can't see, can only touch. They reach out, feel gore. It's rad."

"Have you seen my associate? He has the camera."

"Oh, get their heads, too."

She stepped closer to the dryer, the stack of chicken carcasses, wrapped like presents, piled on top. The bucket at her feet was stained with something dark, its color uncertain under these fluorescent lights. "And then you'll be ready to do the audition tape?"

"Yeah, yeah, yeah."

She turned back to him.

He was gone.

The room seemed to double in size, walls receding as if by dolly zoom.

"Damn it, Jake." She only realized she'd said this aloud when the sound of her voice found the contours of the space, the metallic sides of the washing machine, the exposed cement behind the sink, and echoed back.

The chicken carcasses: she could smell them now, a cloying funk.

She went to the door. Caleb had closed it, or it had closed

on its own accord. She turned the doorknob, inched the door open. Down the hall, two teens were trying to hang a black cloth up in a doorway.

"He said we'd get blood," one said.

"Last year, it was red Kool-Aid. Stained my Vans."

"He said 'blood,' so I dunno. He said like the elevator thing in *The Shining*."

"Never saw it."

Bridget closed the door. She approached the chickens. She knew that inside those clean, neat packages were messes of viscera.

She could do this. She would do this. And then Caleb would do his part. Of all the tasks he could have charged her with, gutting chickens at least seemed somewhat sane, something a real person would do in a real home to prepare a real meal. Except she'd been relegated to this cell of a room, ancillary and out of sight.

She placed her hand flat against the first bundled chicken. She was relieved to feel only the smooth dry paper. She hefted it—its surprising, dense weight—and placed it on top of the washing machine. She turned it over until the seam side was up. She ran her finger beneath the paper, pulled at the masking tape until she could open the bundle like an envelope.

As she opened it, her finger brushed the human-like texture of the defeathered skin. She pulled her hand back, realizing that she'd been expecting the chicken to be cold, but here it was room temperature, which made it harder for her to think of it as meat, the stuff of a barbecue; this had the texture of a living body.

It was on its back, little wings gathered as if in prayer on its chest. Its head was angled unnaturally. There were still stray feathers, the light dusting of down, on its skin. She placed her hand on its sternum, wondered how she was going to remove the organs. Unlike the chickens she'd bought from the grocery store, this one had not yet been gutted. Its body mostly maintained its integrity. She looked around for a knife, a pair of scissors, anything. She saw only a single Bic pen resting on the shelf above her. She picked it up, careful not to let her hands get any of the bird's juices on the shelf, and she held the pen like a dagger. She positioned the nib of the pen in the middle of the bird's chest, then pushed until she felt the scrape of bone. She pushed some more until the pen found its way between bones, into the satisfying sink of meat. She tried to pull down, thinking she could just unzip this thing with her improvised blade, but the resistance was too much for this thin piece of plastic. She pulled the pen out and saw only the small piercing it had left. The hole winked shut. Instead of sawing this thing open, she'd have to try a different approach. She punctured the chest again, this time half an inch below the initial cut. She'd have to open this chicken by perforation.

When she'd put a dozen centimeter-wide holes down the front of the chicken, she put down the pen. On the painted white metal of the washing machine, the pen glowed with a clear viscous something. She placed her fingers on the perforation she'd made in the breast. She pushed her fingers in, each one looking for a different purchase around the breastbone, in the ribs. It hurt. Tiny splinters of bone found her cuticles, insinuated themselves beneath her nail beds. The pain encouraged her to pull more forcefully at the animal, and soon she was feeling the crack of the whole thing opening in her bare hands.

The smell that wafted up into her nostrils was not the fetid odor of a dead thing—she did not retch as she had expected to. Rather, it was something else: a tang that her brain met with the reception of the deprived. Before her, the body of the animal was splayed open, organs presenting themselves as tumescent pearls to pluck. She wrapped her fingers around the bloodied stress ball of what might have been the liver. It fit nicely into her palm.

"There's an easier way to do that, you know."

Dr. Docter was in the doorway. He was still holding his tumbler of whiskey, still barefoot.

His sudden appearance had not startled her. It had distracted her from her task, frustratingly.

She dropped the liver into the bucket. It made a splat.

"Here," he said, stepping forward. The floor was exposed concrete beneath his feet. He pointed with his whiskey hand to the chicken. "Gotta go in at the bottom."

He was now within arm's reach of her. She could have touched his chest, smeared his crisp button-up with viscera.

"Two fingers," he said, demonstrating by holding up his middle and index together. He did have on a wedding band, a black one. Maybe his wife was dead, and this was some sort of mourning band.

He curved his two extended fingers. "Hook her there," he said, gesturing toward the bottom of the carcass. "And pull." He jerked his fingers up. "She'll split pretty quickly, open up for you. Should be able to get wherever you want from there."

She could feel the skin between her fingers drying sticky. "I have my own way."

"Well," he said, crunching ice. His tumbler had acquired ice since she'd last seen him. "Your way is gross."

She responded to her censure the only way she knew how, to assimilate it into a humorless shtick. She held her hands, in a mock grope, up to his face. "Yum, yum," she said, sticking out her tongue.

He waved her away. That was the correct response, the one she knew from Mabel; Jake wouldn't even acknowledge bad jokes. When Mabel had attempted to shoo away her mom's flailing attempts at humor, it had only encouraged Bridget, like she became the kid who craved negative reinforcement. Mabel had once said as much, but Bridget began to think of her flights of obnoxiousness as acts of generosity, a way of offering her daughter an opportunity to shoo her away, an opportunity within the conditions Bridget set. Indeed, Bridget would not have known what to do if Mabel had ever actually laughed.

Dr. Docter said, "You should really remove your ring first."

She still had it on, of course, had never taken it off. Her real engagement ring, sure, but essentially a prop now. People trusted you more when you had one, that's all.

"Eighteen karat?" he said.

She lowered her hands. "Twenty-four."

He smiled, performed some practiced eyebrow accents. "No. Whoever told you twenty-four karat was a liar. Can't make jewelry out of that, too soft. There's gotta be some alloy in there. Your fingers ever turn green?"

"No," she said. "No." She put her hands back into the animal—felt the relief of the warm guts after her fingers had been cooled in the air—and pulled out a jumble of organs. She dropped them into the bucket.

"Should have done what I did." He held up his ring finger, extending it like an incompetent kid who doesn't understand how to flip the bird. "Tungsten carbide."

"Is it heavy? Looks heavy."

He looked at his hand. "It's supposed to be strong, not heavy. But, yes, it is heavier than your average eighteen-karat."

"Why would it need to be strong?"

"Well." This time his performative smirk broke into an

actual smile. "I still don't really know." He set the tumbler down on the nearby shelf and began rolling the ring around his finger.

He leaned against the side of the dryer and explained that when he had been shopping for a wedding band, he spent unmeasurable and unrecoverable hours on internet message boards with names like MensRingsForum and ManJewels.

"So that's what people use the internet for." She recalled Caleb's instruction to remove the heads.

"I was researching the best options. I got sucked into these long debates all about which metals were better. It was weirdly—captivating."

She wrapped her hand around the chicken's neck, felt tendon, the knotted rope of spine.

"I began noticing which posters prioritized scratch resistance, which prioritized strength, which prioritized weight, and which amongst those valued lightweight options and which valued heavier options."

When on a job, providing the dads with an engaged-seeming audience was the most crucial part, and the most taxing part. Indeed, it was their performance—and her providing them the social stages they always desperately craved—that was more important than that of a teen sight-reading bad imitations of bad dialogue, even if it meant suffering through monologues that were more torturous than anything that Nautilus over there could inflict.

She asked, "Why would someone value a heavier ring?"

"To build hand strength."

She yanked, and the chicken's head popped off with surprising ease. What didn't come off as easily was the skin. The head was loose but trapped like a bouncy ball in a condom. She grabbed the Bic pen and began to puncture the neck flesh.

"As I was reading all this stuff," Dr. Docter said, "I was trying to figure out which group I identified with. There were those with Tasmanian Devil avatars advocating for aesthetics."

She dropped the head, with its comet tail of skin, into the bucket. It didn't land with a plop. It landed with a squish, the bottom of the bucket now covered with organs.

"Then there were those championing the highest-temperature resistant options, and their avatars were tiny pictures of their ring fingers, but those also looked like pictures of dicks because the images were small and pixelated."

"Why were you looking all this up? Shouldn't your wife have been doing it?"

"I didn't have my own avatar on the message board, just a translucent gray silhouette selected by default. For some reason this bothered me. I couldn't figure out how to make my little avatar what I wanted, and I couldn't figure out what ring material I wanted. It suddenly seemed to mean so much."

She began unwrapping a new carcass.

"Until I finally landed on tungsten carbide. I felt good about its strength, its scratch resistance." He held up his left hand, moving his ring finger up and down, as if wondering, in the years since, if he'd begun to notice increased strength in his left ring finger.

Except: this couldn't have been years ago. Years ago, there wouldn't have been internet message boards devoted to such niche fetishes. He was talking about something in the last year, two at most.

"What kind your wife get?"

He slid the ring off his finger, twirled it around between thumb and index. "People trust you when they see a ring."

She almost said, "I know." Instead, she focused on the chicken. She tried his method, sliding two fingers into the carcass, pulling up. The hole dilated, purple intestines expanding out.

As soon as she completed this wretched task, she could go find Caleb.

She asked, "Why would anyone need to trust you?"

"It's not what you think."

And as soon as she found Caleb, she could tape his fake audition.

She asked, "Bedside manner?"

"Parents," he said.

And as soon as she taped Caleb's fake auction, she could get this job back on track, wrest control of the night, of everything.

She asked, "You an OB?"

He shook his head, pulled the tumbler from the shelf. "Retired from general practice years ago. Then I picked up this little retirement job. Not for the money. I just discovered that, well, retirement didn't suit me. I need to keep busy, or I—something. Nah, I meant parents of the football players. They're the ones with the sway around here. They're the ones to have on your side. Now I'm just the resident doctor for the overly funded athletics program at Valley Christian Academy, making sure the guys on the team didn't bonk out in the heat. I tend to sprains, shocks, concussions. Make sure everyone's alive enough to get to Nationals."

She unloaded the next chicken into the bucket.

"My penlight has already failed to contract the pupils of enough concussed brains to know these kids will be in deep trouble down the line. But for now, their little successes are bringing in the money to build that new stadium." He finished his drink. "And pay me. Nice thing about the brain—no nerve endings, no pain."

He seemed to contemplate the profound emptiness of his glass.

Above Bridget was a stack of mint-green towels. She reached for one, but before she touched it, Dr. Docter said, "No."

"What?"

"Those are the good towels."

"Where are the bad towels?"

On his way out the door, he said, "We don't have bad towels."

After the other finalists at the OvationNation quarterly contest gave their speeches—one about being the wife of an unnamed member of the Nixon White House implicated in wrongdoing, the other about how the speaker's resemblance to a murderous despot made him nervous to leave his home for over a decade—Bridget had to debate the merits of each speech and decide on a winner with Mr. and Mrs. Dover. For this, they were granted no privacy, no back room in which they could deliberate; they had to huddle right there on the stage. Just off the stage, the Ovationeers mingled, congratulated the speech-givers. After the Dovers finished trying to figure out which senior member of the Nixon White House Joanne Haldeman could have been married to, one of them asked about the Godzilla man. Bridget said she didn't buy it. But he was so charming, one of them said. And he knew all the right words, the other said. That's just it, Bridget said, he was too confident. And, one said, he didn't really look that much like Ivan the Terrible—no, the other interjected, that was the other speech, we're talking about the Godzilla guy. Oh, yes. He was too confident to be believable, Bridget said. But, one responded, I remember that movie, the one that was not *Godzilla*. Yes, the other said, that is a real movie. No, Bridget said, I don't mean that the story is not real, I mean that—his delivery, his performance, it didn't work.

The conclusion, she said, that lesson: it was too pat.

When she'd worked as an extra on that not-Godzilla movie, a couple years before she snagged the part in *In A Pickle*, her father had dropped her off at the set alone. He had some other business to take care of that day. She told him about her slo-mo running faux pas when he picked her up, but she'd never taken any lesson from that moment—she certainly had never lived full speed—and it had not even occurred to her, until the story had been Silly-Puttied into her father's first-person account, that it was worthy of embarrassment. She had not felt embarrassed when that man with the bullhorn had corrected her. She'd merely thought it was funny. But apparently that little anecdote had been reconstituted inside her father's brain as something worthy of shame.

But, one of the Dovers was saying, I found him quite convincing. That's the problem, Bridget said. But, the other was saying, we saw that movie—he wasn't lying about that. It's not the story, Bridget said, it's him. What's the difference? they wanted to know. In the end, her vote for the guy who looked like Ivan the Terrible was outnumbered by their two votes for her father. Before he could return to the podium to accept the gilded microphone trophy, Bridget slipped off the stage for the bathroom. After she finished not-peeing under the disapproving portrait of a bottle-blond Christ, she emerged to find her father. It was unclear if he'd been waiting for the bathroom or for her.

She now walked over to the Docters' laundry room sink. With the heel of her hand, she turned it on. No water came. She kicked the pipe beneath the sink.

She considered grabbing one of the good towels. But she

didn't. She understood, with aching resentment, the sanctity of the good towels. It was periodically heartening to think that Mabel, too, understood such things, and was holding the same line with Tod.

She went to the laundry room door, and with her forearm managed to turn the doorknob. Walking out into the hall—which had already transformed into a dark and hellish corridor, this vibe mostly owing to simple black sheets hung from the walls and strategically placed black lights—she held her viscera-caked hands out in front of her.

Dr. Docter was wrong, she knew, wrong about the brain, wrong that no nerve endings meant no pain. The brain did register pain, but it would manifest years later. She remembered reading about Plato's epistemic spectrum; from the visible realm to the intelligible realm, pain belonged in the visible. Even the bloodless kind of pain was a matter of signals, chemicals. Ultimately, Bridget was a devout Materialist. She knew the physical expenditure of pain would always outweigh the psychic.

● **REC**

The frame focuses first on something like a drained fish tank, its glass opaque with filth, fogged with humidity. When the focus pulls toward something beyond the glass, the tank reveals dozens of little almond-size piñatas hanging from a small ersatz tree. A hand enters the frame and pulls the lid off the tank to get footage of the quivering chrysalises, much more than a dozen, and that same hand reaches in to flick one of them, then slaps the glass wall of the butterflies' habitat.

10.

Bridget made it to the kitchen. The sink was miraculously unbusy. She got the water flowing with a bump of her elbow and lathered up.

Around her, teenagers were wandering in, looking for snacks, drinks, direction. Some of them were carrying props for the haunted house, rubber heads smeared with fake blood, a plastic bag full of vermin snarled with plague.

She dried her hands on the good dish towel hanging off the side of the kitchen island. Using most of the island's countertop was a young woman in a skeleton shirt, sleeves rolled up to the humerus, decorating sugar cookies. The frosting was gathered in a sandwich bag, and she was squeezing it through a fine hole cut in the corner, applying black features to the pumpkin-shaped cookies, a foundational layer of orange having already been shellacked on. The young woman was wearing medical latex gloves to keep her hands clean during this procedure, and her hair was in a ponytail, strands falling out, strands that threatened to get into the wet frosting, a threat that caused her to try to hold her face high above the cookies. This looked uncomfortable.

Bridget asked, "Do you need help?"

The girl looked up. She already had orange frosting on her brow, in that way the youth have of making an error look like a stylistic choice. "Do you know how?"

"I mean." Bridget's urge to prove her fine motor skills to this teenager flared like a rash. "Of course." But: "I need to find Caleb. He's auditioning for me. I'm a casting—"

"Here." She handed Bridget the frosting, warmed by her hand. "Those," she said, pointing to a quadrant of un-faced cookies. "Those need mouths, eyes."

"But do you know where Caleb is? He's auditioning for—do you like *Star Wars*?"

The young woman selected a new sandwich bag already prepared with white frosting. There, beside the box of latex gloves, was a row of frostings, ordered according to Roy G. Biv. She, this young woman, this—

"What's your name?"

"Anya," said Anya.

—this Anya was clearly one of those perfectionists, one of those young women, because they were always young women, who would rather X-Acto-knife a spelling error out of a diary page than to scratch it out or, God forbid, let the error stand. While not one of this breed herself, Bridget seemed to spot them everywhere, in the precision of pens peeking from apron pockets of waitresses, in the collar bones visible like coat hangers holding loose-fitting shirts, and she felt for them, she did, even envied the dedication on display. They were always beautiful, these women, always blind to the advantages they'd already been given. Bridget ran her fingers over both eyebrows and said, "I just need to find Caleb. He's auditioning. I need to put him on tape. It's very important."

"Yes," Anya said, "everything *Caleb* is important, isn't it?" She added a white glimmer of light in the black-circle eye of one jack-o-lantern cookie.

Bridget wondered how a jack-o-lantern's eye, a geometric shape representing an absence, could reflect light. She ached for the dark space of her vanity room.

Anya said, "He'll be voted most likely to be at the center of the next Watergate."

"What?" Bridget said. "What do you mean by that?"

"Please?" Anya pointed her own frosting—the tip leaking a pearl of white—at the cookies Bridget was neglecting.

Bridget got to work, adding half-moon eyes to one. Holding her hands steady, she could almost hear Mabel's voice offering a pointed critique of her linework. Mabel had once sent an entire trayful of Christmas cookies down the garbage disposal because, she said over the noise of the disposal, Santa's face came out like he had elephantiasis.

Bridget said, "But what did you mean? Watergate."

"1972," Anya said. "Nixon? AP Gov."

"I mean, why Caleb?"

"He's a con artist," she said.

"Well." Bridget struggled to draw the right mouth shape. "He's an actor. He's going to be famous. If I can find him."

"And here we got Anna jizzing on some cookies." This voice—like a trebly speaker just starting to break up—was from a guy obscured by a video camera. He was getting the camera right up to Anya's work, so much so that the cameraman's elbow smeared the frosting of a cookie.

Anya shouted, "Skylar!"

He pushed the camera even closer, and Anya gently pushed it back. He had a knotted ponytail.

"Hey!" he said, lowering the camera. "That hurt my eye!"

"No, I didn't."

"You could have! You could have hurt my camera." He held the Panasonic DV Pro in both hands like a baby.

"Excuse me," Bridget said, a fission of panic in her professional tone. "Excuse me."

Skylar was ignoring her for the more tantalizing prospect of harassing Anya. He had a light sketching of a mustache, a vague idea of one. Bridget reached out—toward the camera or Skylar, she wasn't entirely sure—her hand briefly touching the camera, her camera, before landing on, and taking firm hold of, Skylar's wrist.

"Hey!" He tried to twist away from her. His other hand protected the camera. "Anna, get your mom off me!"

Bridget was apparently gripping his wrist pretty firmly. But this was her camera. She'd bought it. It was hers.

"Where did you get this?" she said, hearing her voice come out calm and inquisitive, even as she was wrestling this teenager's sinewy limbs.

Skylar finally freed himself, but in doing so he lost hold of the camera. The little black machine took flight over Anya's head. It landed—not with a crash and burst of lens glass but with a slap of plastic on skin—in Caleb's hands. He cradled it like a football.

"Caleb!" Bridget said. She rushed up to him, alarmed anew by his height over her. She still thought of height as correlating to age and experience. It mostly tracked, since she was still taller than Jake and Mabel, but standing now before Caleb, her eyes at armpit level, she felt like a shriveled crone. "I took care of the chickens. They're gutted, ready for the—whatever. So I'm thinking—good catch, by the way—we go over the scene a couple times, make sure you have it down, then put it to tape."

Caleb was looking over the camera. He had the air of a *2001* ape examining the lethal possibility of a femur for the first time.

Bridget said, "Seriously, if you'd dropped that camera, we'd have no audition. So, okay—"

"Hey, so that's like not actually mine," Skylar said behind

her, his voice muffled with—

"Cookies!" Anya shouted. "Those are my cookies!"

Skylar continued: "I think I'm supposed to give that camera back to that kid."

Bridget turned to see the cookie and camera thief now trying to swipe a frosting tube from the counter, Anya swatting at his hands while trying to gather the unmolested cookies onto a plate.

"Where?" Bridget said. "Where did you see him? The kid you said. The kid you got the camera from."

"Who, Brian?" Skylar's tongue was orange.

"Ryan," Bridget said, only now remembering the name of Jake's character. "My associate. Where is he?"

"Skylar, eat a dick!" Anya said on her way out of the kitchen.

Bridget turned back to Caleb, put her hand on his arm, as if that could keep him from disappearing again. "Stay."

Caleb handed the camera to the bystanders in the kitchen. "Pass it around."

Skylar said, "He's on the roof, I think."

"The roof?" She turned back to Caleb. "Just don't mess with the camera!"

Skylar said, "Yeah, setting up with the Tonies."

Caleb said, "We're gathering blackmail material tonight!" A few no-names laughed at this, and Caleb gestured at the camera. "Pass it around!"

To Skylar, Bridget said, "He can't be on the roof. He gets vertigo."

Skylar shrugged, wiped some frosting from his chin. "He is."

Bridget tried to swipe the camera back from a kid in blond dreadlocks too dumb to be a costume, but he was too agile.

To Caleb, she said, "Stay here. With the camera." And she

ran into the living room.

The room was almost entirely dark, black sheets having been hung over the windows, the only light coming from the projection TV showing a swirl of lights that looked like the underside of your eyelids when you rubbed the heel of your hands against them. The music playing through unseen speakers was a throbbing headache, and the other bodies in the room were wraithlike absences of light, noticeable only when they moved.

When her body collided with something, though, it wasn't the pliable something of a body but cracking plastic obstructing her shins. She fell face-first into what seemed to be a kiddie pool full of—something. Something just tepid enough to be unsettling. Something vaguely redolent of vinegar, an acidity now making its way through her sinuses as she pushed her face up and spat, something that had gooey balls floating in it like bubble tea.

Pulling herself out of the kiddie pool, weirdly worried about what must have splashed onto the carpet, her eyes began adjusting to the darkened room. Floating in the pool were eyeballs; the liquid was something approximating blood. She suppressed a retch, then reminded herself that this was surely some concoction stewed up with sundries from the pantry.

The fake blood was oozing into her underwear. She got to her feet, helped by the darkened figure of a boy offering aid or maybe just a beer.

In the foyer, she found light. There was the small chandelier that hung like a bright idea, but there was also the dusk outside flaring orange and purple. Her wet feet squished a bit on the tile floor. Whatever she'd fallen into had the consistency more of cheap wine than of blood. Maybe it really was wine. She licked her finger, detected something astringent, tannic, notes of cherry. In her hand, she found something squishy, like a stress ball. It was an eye. It looked real enough. Dilated pupil ringed with an iris of blue, the surrounding white fissured with red.

She opened the front door, ran outside. Around the front lawn, which was actually some landscaped arrangement of spiky plants emerging from wood chips, some kids were trying to tape up a yellow police line. Another was making chalk outlines on the cement, drawing around the body of a buddy who wasn't staying still enough.

Out on the sidewalk, she looked up to the roof. From this angle she still couldn't see anyone up there. She kept walking back, into the cul-de-sac, to get a better angle, until finally she saw: Her son, standing on the gabled roof above the garage. He was holding a bale of white fuzz, peeling off handfuls and handing it, alternatingly, to a boy and a girl. They were stretching out the fuzz until it became diaphanous and cobwebby, then applying it to the second-story windows. Jake looked sure-footed up there on the roof, confident in his task, in his contribution to the project. He had the reassuring movements of a gaffer.

When he handed some more cobweb fuzz to the girl, she said something to him. Bridget was too far away to hear the exact words, but she could make out the light, teasing tone. Jake's body did something she'd never seen before: it seemed to bow as if physically receiving the jest, and then straighten as if expelling it. He said something in response, and Bridget held her breath, certain that Jake was responding to a friendly tease with defensive aggression. She closed her eyes, imagining her son screaming at two strangers on the roof of the Docters' mini-mansion, the way his voice would rise when his eyes threatened tears, the way he tried to cover up his emotions by folding his arms across his heaving chest, as if to hold himself down. She figured it would only be a matter of moments before he wound up insulting everyone, marks included, and she'd have to rush up there herself, smooth things over.

But whatever Jake said was received with a little scream of laughter. Bridget opened her eyes. Jake was smiling at this reception. Whatever was going on, things were working. The boy now joined in. The three of them, they were all just: joking around. Peers socializing. Exchanging comments with the intent to amuse not berate. She desperately wanted to get closer, to hear what they were saying, to know the particulars of how Jake was sharing a simple joke with these kids. But she was also terrified to know. She'd never gotten the chance to see him with friends, not after they'd left Denver. He was a high school graduate now—technically, equivalently—and she'd never seen him hang out with friends at the age when hanging out began to take on an element of performance art, a way of being in the world that was at once a commentary on the world and a commentary on the very construct of hanging out. She'd never had a chance to see that. She always imagined the moment when she'd drive him somewhere and he'd insist that she drop him off a block early, tacitly telling her this was his space, not hers. She longed for that moment of rejection.

What if they scrapped the whole plan and stayed here? Jake wouldn't have to go home. Here were peers, friends. Here were people who could affirm whatever weird passions and interests he felt compelled to hide from her within the claustrophobic walls of a motel room. What if she changed plans altogether, made a play for Dr. Docter, positioned herself as wife number two. She could make that happen, could make an angle for Jake to continue whatever stupid joke had now passed.

The three of them up there were back to work, Jake dutifully handing gauzy messes to the two. Soon, they were making their delicate way up to the next tier of the roof. Odd to see them move so carefully, these teenage creatures for whom care was anathema. The girl held out her hand for support as she was lifting herself up, and Jake took it, kept her steady.

Making a play for Dr. Docter would be a long con, something she'd never done before. The kind of long con you'd have to live, the kind without the sharp heel-turn she was accustomed to. The endgame would be to make something sustainable. Making a life was the ultimate long con, and she wasn't sure she had what it took to do that, not again. But she could try. Because that was the only choice she had. That was the only way she knew how to make anything happen: Force herself into a position in which there was no other choice. Success was the only escape. She could do it because she had to do it.

Behind her a car gave a gentle, tapping honk. She turned and got out of the way, watched the black Ford Bronco make its way to the house.

Bridget walked to the sidewalk, about ninety degrees around the cul-de-sac from the Docters' house. She sat on the curb, which sloped down to the street. Beside her, one of the Docters' neighbors had a box waiting on their porch labeled The Good Wine Club. Surely that was the level of comfort everyone aspired to, when booze could just appear on your doorstep, when all pretense to responsibility—even a responsibility to being a crook—slipped away, replaced by home deliveries of your vice. She imagined all those celebrities who'd slunk away into reclusiveness had built up enough capital to just sedate themselves for as long as they wanted. They probably lazed in giant beds with thousand thread-count sheets that felt like wombs. All ambitions were surely just a means to that end. It didn't matter if your means were more traditional forms of human endeavor, didn't matter how many mini-mansions you occupied along the way, or how many turquoise-inlaid hubcaps you could afford for your Bronco, it was all bent toward *that*, a return to the womb, to be squishy and free of worry.

Behind the Docters' house, meanwhile, the sun was fighting its way down, resisting tooth and flaming nail. Flaring angrily across the sky, it was reminding the world that it'd be missed when gone.

Bridget stood up, remembering that this was a gated community, patrolled by people with plastic stun guns and no training. Surely what she was doing—and what was that, quietly contemplating taking Dr. Docters' money, either by hook-up or crook-up—was loitering, and she didn't want to attract any attention.

Making her way back to the Docters' house—where she realized she'd have to find Caleb again—she told herself she should leave Jake here to make friends, that it was the least she could do for him.

Two decades ago, outside the bathroom outside the nave of a church, she saw her father for the last time. He was holding his trophy, gripping the gilded microphone. When she'd opened the door to find him in the hallway, he seemed unfazed, as if he'd been waiting for her, but he said, Oh, hello. And she said something. And he said something. And it was distressingly fine. He asked how college was going, and she said fine, recalling the burden of self-reporting your own life, the impulse to just *fine* something away, though this time she could see the disappointment register on her father's face, the way he took her *fine* to be a roadblock, and he said that's nice and she didn't ask him why he'd taken her story, made it into his own, because all the anger that had coiled hot inside her when she'd been in the bathroom now dissipated like a breath into the modest belfry above, and she panicked for a moment, looking for it, trying to recapture the sense of indignity that had sent her scurrying to the bathroom in the first place, to hide from the sight of this man claiming an award for claiming her life, when right now in the beige hallway bordering the nave, he held the cheap thing and she could see the seams of its plastic coating, and then more urgent needs asserted themselves, and he motioned that he needed to use the restroom, and she let him pass, while he took the trophy in with him and closed the door. And she left, went back to Layla's and watered her plants.

Years later, when Jake came home from Griffin-Dowd Middle School saying he needed to write and perform a monologue and he needed her help, their brainstorming session soon evolved into her telling him stories from her life that were malleable enough to fit the prompt. When she told the story about running in slow motion, she found herself cribbing some details from what she now remembered from her father's award-winning speech that night at OvationNation. These revisions included that little lesson-like tag at the end, which made Jake, even at that age—then a *young* twelve—wince. Still, that monologue earned Jake high praise from his drama teacher, who later commented on how it was nice to see Jake's social confidence developing. By then, Bridget no longer had a clear grasp on what was hers, what was her father's, or what was Jake's.

On Dr. Docter's roof, Jake and the other two—the Tonies, presumably—were already out of sight. On the shrubbery, the yellow police line was taut, impressive. On the sidewalk, the chalk outline was modernist, grim. Blocking the driveway, the black Ford Bronco was oblique, obstructionist.

She stopped within an arm's reach of the car.

The recognition of it pulled out her spine like a rip cord.

It appeared at a distance, as if through the wrong end of binoculars.

The Ford Bronco was empty, she was pretty sure. She moved her legs with the intent to both retreat from, and advance toward, the Bronco. To both hide from it and confirm that it was empty. Each leg took one of those orders, and she nearly collapsed. One leg, whichever was the more competent of the two, caught her, and whipped the other into action.

She ran. Some dumb instinct guided her not out into the street but off at an angle, like a deer darting back and forth to evade a predator. Indeed, around the time she ducked behind the hedge of the neighbor who'd subscribed to The Good Wine Club, she realized that such a mad dash away from the Docters' house was probably the exact wrong thing to do when attempting to avoid being seen by the person who'd driven here in that Bronco with the turquoise-inlaid hubcaps. Maybe, hopefully, it had been Bertram's wife, Ethan's mom. Bridget had never met her, so she'd never be able to place Bridget. But that was stupid. Why else would that car arrive here if not for the haunted house, and who else would come for that haunted house in that car but Ethan from Claymont? And whether or not he'd been driven here by Bertram, his mom, or Santa Claus, he could place her. He *would* place her. In a second.

She looked back over the hedge as if peeking out from a trench. No sign of Ethan and Bertram Cline from Claymont.

And why hadn't she and Jake gone farther from Claymont? She knew they should have put more distance between their last mark and this one.

She peeked out again. No sign of Jake.

They needed to leave. She needed to leave. Now.

Surely she couldn't just leave him here. If she did, though, if she did let him stay with friendly peers rather than an itinerant criminal, might it not be for his own benefit? Wasn't this what he wanted? A normal life-type life? Unless leaving him here (and it would just be for a little bit; she could drive to safety, come back later, and walk up to the house only when she saw that the Bronco had left) was leaving him in harm's way to take the fall for her actions, as if being the kid of a parent was anything else. But no—he'd be safe. He'd spoken to Bertram on the phone, sure, but he'd only gone to their house as a delivery guy, and they'd never spot him from that. She couldn't, though. Even if leaving him meant freeing him, even temporarily, from the custody of a criminal, it also meant leaving him in the mess she'd made for him.

She got to her knees, ready to scoot away with her head below the line of sight. Thank God this gated community didn't have aggressive rules regulating the height of hedges, because this one was currently saving her life.

He'd be fine. He'd understand.

"Miss."

She saw a pair of slippers, pale ankles emerging from those slippers, ankles that turned into spotted calf muscles that disappeared into a robe.

"Miss," the man said again. Behind him, The Good Wine Club box was open. In his hand, a green bottle. She didn't dare raise her eyes any higher, up to his face. He said something in German that sounded like he was calling a rottweiler to attack.

● **REC**

The image blinks. Space-time is torn and sutured, torn and sutured. You're now in the lap of a young man, himself in the lap of what appears to be a papasan chair, and he repeatedly but lovingly blows plumes of pot smoke into the frame. Time passes like this. But then another's voice is asking for the camera back, pleading, saying that it's his, which elicits laughter, and it feels like you're being tucked away into a pocket, only dark jersey material visible.

11.

"Gewürz!"

"What?"

Bridget was in a low squat, both to avoid detection over the hedge of this neighbor, but also to brace herself for whatever this man was calling on.

"Gewürztraminer," he said. "Do you like it?" He extended the bottle he was holding, a white wine.

"Oh." She relaxed a bit, but she still couldn't risk being seen over the hedge, so before standing fully erect, she moved to be obscured by a column. "Gewürztraminer," she said, "sure."

"It's just too *something* for my liking." He was nodding like a bobblehead, either by agreement or neurology she wasn't sure. "You know? Too *something?*"

"Everything is too something."

"Isn't it." He looked into the open box of wine. "I used to gravitate *toward* things. At some point, my magnetization switched, and now I'm guided by repulsion. I just gravitate toward the things I'm least repulsed by. Here, take it."

He looked at her. She could see the assessment behind his eyes, like the way the Terminator scanned each part of a person's body for size, shape, utility. She'd enjoyed watching that one with Jake in their motel the other night, enjoyed throwing bologna slices from their Subway sandwiches at the screen during the climactic scenes; the pleasures of motel life came not from the replication of home, but from the things you'd never allow yourself to do at home.

"You gonna enjoy this with a fella?" He insinuated the bottle of wine into her hands.

"Yes," she said. She held up her hand, saw a fleck of chicken goop stuck to a side stone of her ring.

"What's the lucky man's name?" His brow did something tectonic above his eyes.

"Jake," she said.

"Hmph." Somehow his smile became a frown without any perceptible movement in his face. "Not a name for an adult. When grown, a Jake should be a Jacob."

"I'll let him know." She said this in a tone of gratitude, as if he'd bestowed upon her a genuinely interesting fact about worms having two brains or Sweden having four official languages.

He nodded, surely just happy to have interacted with another person today.

She held up the bottle, said, "Thank you," and backed away slowly, as if from a badger that had mysteriously emerged from a sewer.

As she moved away from this man's house, bottle of wine in hand, her eyes were on that Bronco wedged into the Docters' driveway. With the sun now gone, leaving only smears of itself above, she moved toward her car only in the dark patches of street, avoiding the streetlamps' copper wedges of light.

Maybe she'd go park in some isolated corner of this neighborhood, keep herself company with this wine, until the Bronco had left. Or maybe it'd be best to just go back to the motel for a bit.

When she got to her car, her key was already out, pointed. She was able to get into the car quickly, but noticed that her driver's seat was in a patch of light. She turned the engine over—the radio turned on—and she backed up until she felt the pall of darkness over her face.

She steadied her hands on the screw-top of the Gewürztraminer. She twisted it, felt the seal crack in her hands.

Fact was, she had to go. It wasn't a choice, really. She was in danger. Jake was not. Parents left their kids at other houses all the time. The kids preferred that. Jake hadn't socialized with a peer in ages—surely, he'd be relieved to see that she'd gone. Those were just facts.

The man in the robe had been right—this wine really was too *something*. Didn't help that it wasn't chilled, but it was cloying, like her mother's Sunday perfume.

The car was suddenly sliding backwards. Her foot had slid off the brake, and the car was apparently still in reverse. She pressed down, but her foot landed on the accelerator, not the brake, and the car lurched back. A thud, followed by a minor explosion of aluminum and plastic, told her she'd backed into the recycling bin someone had taken out to the curb, but it was enough to shoot adrenaline into her heart, and soon she was pulling a screeching U-turn out of the Docters' cul-de-sac.

She almost made it, too. She almost made it out of the neighborhood, back onto the highway, back to her shitty motel room where she could drink the entirety of the gross room-temperature wine and pass out. She almost did. But she didn't. Instead, she idled at the corner stop sign positioned just before the exit from the gated community. The guard who'd let her in was no longer there, his little booth dark. The gate beside the booth was simple, black metal, each post sharpened to a skyward point. The more she stared at these moon-glinted tips, the more it felt like a medieval battlement. She could imagine the unwashed trying to storm this exurban Jericho. Boiled oil poured over heads. She looked up, saw only the speckles of bug guts on her windshield mingling with the stars emerging beyond.

She offered the stars choice curses.

Jake would not be fine. Not back there, not anywhere.

She took another swig of wine.

The bike patrol was loitering in her headlights, fifteen feet away, twenty. A man-child in an ill-fitting uniform, gripping the handlebars. Staring her down as if in a standoff. He put his right foot on the pedal, steered, wobblingly, over to her driver's side window. He motioned for her to roll it down. She obeyed.

"What ya got there?" he said.

"Nothing, officer."

"You a guest of the Docters?"

"My name is on the list—Cline."

He nodded. "I'm not an officer." He leaned forward, looking toward the bottle between her legs. "Party, huh?"

"Just a little one. For the kids."

He tried to lean even closer, but this disrupted the balance of his bike, and he had to step forward to keep from tipping over onto the side of her car. He righted himself. "Maybe I'll stop by."

She smiled, nodded.

"*After* my shift."

"You already got the costume, right?" She pointed at his uniform. The staccato rhythm of her chuckle offered cover for her rapid heartbeat, shortness of breath.

He leaned back, appeared to want some time to decide if her comment had been offensive or innocuous. "Well. Best get back to the party then."

He pedaled away. The night was silent except for the squeak of his unoiled gears.

The path to the exit was now unobstructed. Surely those gates would part as she approached, motion-sensored or what-have-you.

Nothing said she didn't belong here quite like metal gates, even if she was looking at them from the inside. Their Denver house had a security system called GATE, which she accidentally tripped so many times the operator she had to call to disarm it knew her affectionately as "B," though when Mabel was around, her daughter could always remember the code and intervene.

She took another swig of wine, simply because her mouth had gone dry with nerves, and she pulled a U-turn, headed back toward the cul-de-sac.

She was nervous but the wine was working.

She parked at the delta of the street, beside a cluster of scarecrows losing their straw to the wind. She made sure the car was facing the exit gate.

She got out of the car. Wine bottle in hand, she walked toward the end of the cul-de-sac. As the Clines' Bronco came into view, she tried to hug the edge of the sidewalk where trees offered coverage from the streetlamp.

Her goal was now simple, blissfully stripped of all ambition: Just get Jake and go. Whatever she'd hoped she could get out of the Docters she now had to leave on the table. She just needed her son.

Close enough to read the Bronco's license place, she stopped. She couldn't just walk in the front door, snatch Jake and leave. From the look of the place, the lights in the front windows, the guests were all congregating around the front of the house, still setting up the decorations. If she were to go in the front door, the chances of her running into Ethan or Bertram or both would be too high.

She ducked down the paved path that ran between the Docters' house and their neighbor's house. It wended around the Docters' house where, in the backyard, it sloped down and led below a deck. This was where they kept their trash cans, and on the deck above she could see a couple of people milling about, smoking, from the smell of it. Listening to them debate about whether it was better to be eaten by a shark or a bear, she figured neither was Ethan or Bertram.

This was the ingress she needed, a way to sneak covertly back into the house, find Jake without attracting the kind of attention that going in the front door would attract. She came out from under the deck and went up the stairs. The two young men smoking on the deck looked younger than they'd sounded. They were starting to come to a rapprochement on the topic, agreeing that when attacked by a shark the possibility of drowning would ease the pain of death. They regarded her briefly and blankly.

She hesitated in view of the sliding glass door. It led into the dining room, with a view of the kitchen, and people were assembling in there, moving a couple CPR dummies onto the island and starting to outfit them as victims of a zombie-mauling. She couldn't make out the faces of all involved, didn't want to risk one of them being Ethan.

She turned back to the smokers. "Can I bum one of those?"

One of them hid his cigarette behind his back. The other just looked at his as if it had appeared by surprise in his hand. "Aren't you, like, working?" This from the guy who didn't attempt to hide his cigarette; he must have been the one with the pack.

She smoothed the front of her theater blacks. "Fifteen-minute break," she said.

He took a pack from his pocket. "Trade?" He nodded to the bottle of wine in her hand.

She handed it over and accepted the pack of cigarettes. The two guys drank from the bottle ambitiously, as if it would evaporate if not consumed entirely, immediately. She pulled a cigarette from the pack, remembered that she didn't actually smoke.

After a belch that seemed to ripple the air, the lead smoker said, "Isn't catering supposed to just go through the side door?" He nodded behind him.

Bridget felt flecks of tobacco cling to her sweaty palms and tried to brush them away. "I—was just looking for that, yes. Got a little lost."

His oblique nod seemed to be toward the other side of the house, away from the path that had led her here. She popped the cigarette into her mouth. The guy extended a lighter, flicked it on, and held the little flame in his palm like a miracle. She leaned forward and inhaled the flame into her cigarette. The smoke in her lungs felt oddly expansive. She coughed out a "Thanks" and went back down the deck stairs.

Down on the grass, she scanned the yard. It disappeared into a darkness that was alien. She expected a backyard to be blasted by light, the contours of the property clearly defined—if not by intention, then at least by the ambient light of the neighborhood. But this neighborhood was different. Here, they could afford darkness.

Looking back up at the house, she took a drag from the cigarette, blew the smoke up into the light from the kitchen window. The smoke demonstrated for her eye the parameters of the light, gave it shape and purpose. She'd be a smoker, she decided.

She went around to the other side of the house, past a covered hot tub and a storage shed with its door ajar. She stopped, peeked into the shed. She couldn't see anything, but she could smell the loamy sweetness of tools caked with cut grass and dried chunks of soil.

She continued around the corner of the house, saw a narrow cement path leading back up to the front of the house, and about halfway up: the glint of glass. She approached it, a door coming into focus. It had a small window in the top half, no lights on inside. It did not seem to be in much use tonight. No one was coming or going through this door. Maybe they hadn't even ordered catering. She placed her hand on the doorknob. It was locked. She put her hands and face to the window, saw nothing but her own distorted reflection.

She threw the cigarette at the door. The spark of embers bouncing off it was aesthetically satisfying if functionally useless to her goal.

She walked back down to the toolshed. Inside, she groped around in the darkness. Her hands grazed the points of a pitchfork, their dry texture of rust; the beaky blades of shears; the scoop of a shovel. She just needed something simple, something she could jimmy that door open with. And she found it when her hands felt a bucket with worn wood handles poking out. She pulled out a small trowel, its blade a subtle diamond shape. She turned back to the shed door just as it closed with a slam. Then she heard the sound of an exterior latch being slid into place.

In college, the year after that summer at Layla's, Bridget took a film course that mostly involved sitting in a dark space, waiting. The course was taught by a popular film critic. The popular film critic, who'd famously abandoned an academic career to champion art both high and low in the syndicated periodicals of America, would visit Boulder periodically just for this course, which examined a single film for the entire semester. The semester-long course was fifteen three-hour class sessions, and the film was divided evenly across those sessions. That meant this semester's film—William Wyler's *Roman Holiday*—and its one hundred and eighteen minutes were diced up until each class meeting viewed and discussed between seven and eight minutes of the film. *Discuss* was not quite accurate, though. Over a three-hour class, they would watch that week's seven-minute segment at various speeds, everyone poring over each frame with Talmudic intensity. At first, Bridget did not think that this particular film—about a bored princess who falls for an American newspaper man while in Rome—was worthy of such scrutiny. It was a light, funny film, a well-made confection that had grown in esteem over the years simply because of the increasing dearth of well-made confections. Audrey Hepburn and Gregory Peck were charming; the locale was lovely to look at, and that was about it. But a funny thing happened: When the popular film critic slowed the first segment of film down, pausing in odd moments to question the triangulation of blocking, composition, and human gesture, something else began to suggest itself. It became something like that Zapruder film, the one that defined the opportunities her mother had stolen from her. Any gesture, frozen on the screen, became pregnant with possibility, and so became sinister. Guiding the students through a slightly blurred freeze-frame of Audrey Hepburn's face, the popular film critic said everyone knew what Barthes had said of Hepburn's face, that it reflected the themes of woman-as-child, woman-as-cat, but here we see woman-as-ghoul. Distortion flickered around her nose in the frozen image, lateral bars of pixels that twitched as if trying to break out of the freeze-frame. Then, unclear if the subject of his thought was the film or the mode of seeing, he said that when you slow any film down enough, it becomes a film about death. And it was after that particular class that the popular film critic caught Bridget on her way out into the hall, said he knew her, that he knew her work, unclear if that second clause was an expansion on or a correction of the first. He then invited her to join him for a drink, and when she said she wasn't twenty-one yet, he said that his mind was already in Cannes, where he was headed as soon as the semester was over, where such a trifling question of age was no question at all, and as he took her arm she felt her body slow, Hepburn in stasis.

In total darkness, she heard, "Keeps blowing open." The voice, just outside the toolshed, was Dr. Docter's. He continued: "So the plan is to run the zipline down from the roof."

Another man's voice said, "It won't tangle with power lines?" This, she knew, was Bertram.

"All our power lines are buried here."

She placed her hands against the door of the toolshed, found fleeting safety in the smooth tactile experience of its cold aluminum. She held her breath.

Dr. Docter's voice continued: "But when I told the HOA about it, they said it would be a blight. So I figure you send them a note on your firm's letterhead, some legalese, a nice way of saying 'Get lost.' You think you can do that for me?"

"I'd be delighted," Bertram said.

Chortles and back slaps dimming in volume told her they were walking away.

She exhaled. She took in deep lungfuls of the toolshed, the dried clay and stale earth. She had the trowel in her hand. She waited another minute before fitting its thin blade between the double doors, searching for the exterior latch. She felt its delicate resistance. She flipped the trowel up and felt the doors ease open.

She emerged from the toolshed cautiously, confirming the empty yard before scooting around the corner of the house and ducking back into darkness.

She returned to that side door and immediately got to work on the lock. The trowel was no use, of course, on the keyhole, couldn't fit into the sliver between door and jamb, so it was only a matter of seconds before she applied its sharp efficacy to a more vulnerable point: She stabbed the blade of the trowel through the window.

The shatter of glass wasn't explosive. It was a delicate tinkle, kindly discreet. She reached through, careful to avoid the teeth of broken glass around the open maw of the window, and unlocked the door from the inside.

Sliding the door open, she kicked the glass on the floor out of the way. The scrape of those shards told her that the floor was cement. This wasn't a side entrance. This was the basement entrance. She reached around, felt the wall just inside the door until her fingers found the light switch. She flipped it. The lights came on dim, hesitant in the way they blinked awake.

The basement didn't so much appear before her; the room didn't come into focus as one space. Rather, there was one object that appeared first, the rest of the space blurrily framing it. It was a coffin.

A simple pine box, painted black, it was a tapered hexagon resting on a folding table.

"Jesus," she said.

For the haunted house, she thought. Hopefully.

She approached it, touched the top. It had recently been painted, the tackiness of not-fully-dried acrylic. She moved her hand to the side, started to push against it just slightly. Figured she could gauge the weight with just a little nudge. Not that she thought there could be a body in there. It was just something for the haunted house, a prop. But there could have been *something* in there. She just wanted to check—a dummy maybe.

The coffin shifted easily against her weight. It was empty.

Just beyond the coffin, an unfinished staircase. At the top, a closed door. Beyond the door, the traffic of teenagers. She crept up the stairs, sensitive to the creaks and complaints of wood and joint. At the top of the stairs, she listened at the door for her son. If only he were loitering just on the other side of the door, she could open it a crack, grab him, and be gone. But she couldn't place his voice in the din. When he and Mabel were babies—and she'd haul them both to Baby Time at the local library, where one corner of the children's reading room was outfitted with throw pillows and a saintly librarian would read board books to kids still figuring out object permanence—she and the other exhausted moms would sit against the wall and not bother with small talk. During those free babysitting sessions, she was amazed at how instantly she knew the wail of one of her children. The particular timbre of a tiny Jake or a tiny Mabel cut through the world to her brain like a telegraph. Listening now at the door, she did recognize a voice, but it wasn't that of her son. Just on the other side of this door, a kid was asking if there was a PlayStation—it was Ethan.

She moved slowly down the stairs, backwards, keeping her eye on the door.

When she got to the bottom of the stairs, a possibility occurred to her, something terrifying: Bertram had told Dr. Docter. Since the two were social with each other, they could have gotten to talking, realized they'd been fed the same story, by the same lady. Maybe by now Dr. Docter had put it together, that he had the culprit in his house.

Her fingernails pressed into the gummy acrylic of the coffin, crescent smiles in black.

But maybe not, maybe rich people were too embarrassed to admit when they'd been had, been taken advantage of, were ashamed enough to keep those secrets safe. Maybe Bertram and Dr. Docter were the type of guy friends who only shared their successes, mythologized the ways the world bent to their gravities; maybe they kept the rest hidden, hidden in places like this, this not-quite-basement filled with a homemade coffin, a deflated air mattress, bikes hanging by their wheels from ceiling hooks, spare chairs stacked in Tetris-like arrangements, a folding futon, a brown dress form, a box for a new television, a pale and plump stomach.

She stepped back until she felt the glass beneath her feet.

It, the stomach, sat there in an unzipped lacrosse bag, a bulky thing. Nested in the bag like a Cabbage Patch doll, it wasn't just a belly; it was a pregnant belly. It was something severed bloodlessly from a body. As she approached it, she could see it was a perfectly round stomach, its belly button even distended, its flesh pale and supple, but attached to no human torso.

Her hand was on it, its uncanny flesh cold like rubber but responsive beneath her touch. She reached her hands all the way into the bag, felt the edges of the stomach, two flesh-tone straps emerging from its sides. On the underside she felt a border: a rubber encasement, sealing the back of this prosthetic.

She pulled her hand back, half expecting to see it covered in the smear of viscera. Instead, in the orange light of the basement, she saw only her own dry skin.

"Oh, here you are."

She turned. Dr. Docter was standing at the foot of the stairs. "Find any fun secrets?"

● **REC**

It's unclear if this strobing is something like a fan passing before a single source of light or if it's an actual strobe. Either way, when bodies begin moving through it, there's the zoetrope effect of trying to see someone through slats in a fence while running past: real movement diced into static bits and reconstituted into an illusion of movement.

12.

Bridget stood up, realizing that she'd been crouched over the bag with the stomach.

"I wasn't snooping."

Dr. Docter gave a performative roll of his eyes. "Why not?"

She stepped toward him, away from the bag. The coffin was between them. "Just not interested. I, uh, need to see if Caleb is ready. To tape his audition. Is he available now?"

He leaned over the coffin like it was a bar top. "Come on. You're not interested? Sarah, I must say, I'm a little hurt. I don't pique your curiosity?"

She placed her hands on the coffin. "This is quite something."

He tapped the top of the coffin with his knuckle. "Out of something comes nothing. A big box to hold nothing."

"Empty?"

"I didn't say that. I said it's the box we become nothing in."

"You have a way with words."

"I do have my way, yes."

She removed her hands from the coffin, took half a step back. She said, "By something, I meant upstairs. The haunted house. You do this every year?"

He backed away from the coffin, sat on the first step. "Since Cheryl died, yes."

"I'm sorry."

"I said," he said, louder, "'Since Cheryl died.'"

"Yes, I heard. Sorry, I meant 'I'm sorry' as in I'm just sorry. Not like I didn't hear."

"Well." He watched the floor between his bare feet. "It bears repeating, I suppose."

She wondered if he was blocking the stairs on purpose.

To the mess on the floor, he said, "This glass?" His toes curled.

"Yes," she said, too quickly. "I saw—that kid Skylar. I heard him say he was looking for liquor."

He looked at her with wide drunken eyes. "Well, he must have missed the bottles I put out upstairs. Dumb kid, huh?"

"Yeah. I'll get a broom." She busied herself in the cluttered shelves, the sleeping bags and the cans of food for emergencies and the Ziploc bag of old batteries leaking battery acid, chalky and calcified. "Have you seen—my associate? Brian?"

"Does it shock you that I provide alcohol for minors?"

She shrugged, her back to him. "Miners need refreshment, too. After all day in the mines, they're bound to be thirsty."

"His name is Ryan, by the way."

"Who?"

"Your associate introduced himself as Ryan, not Brian."

She turned around, busied her hands by straightening imaginary creases in her shirt. She could handle anything, except for being caught in a small error, as she knew where that first felled domino led. The vertiginous feeling was familiar: It wasn't so much that the world got small and retreated from her, but that she shrank from it, became an ineffectual toy, easily plucked up, discarded. "That was a joke," she said. "Miner like a coal miner." She needed to make it up those stairs before she fainted, find Jake before anyone else did. "I'll get a broom upstairs, clean up this glass. You should stay here. With all this glass, it's too dangerous for you to walk around with no shoes."

He picked up a finger-size shard of glass.

She stood before him, making small movements to show she needed to get by, to get up the stairs.

"I meant Ryan," she said. "I'm pretty sure I actually said Ryan, in fact." She could hear a vibrato starting to play in her voice.

He stood up, still holding the piece of glass between thumb and forefinger. "I came down here for something." He pushed past her, over to the foot of the coffin, placed one hand on it, held the glass up with the other, examined it in the light. He looked toward the ceiling. "Turning into a real thing up there."

The stairs were clear for her, but she felt like she needed his permission to leave. "I have—trouble with *r* sounds. It's a thing."

"There's some people you should meet up there."

People: she remembered Bertram's voice, just outside that toolshed, saying he'd be delighted, his tone acquiring an ophidian hiss in her memory. "I'm not feeling too social," she said. "Just looking for my associate."

"Brian."

She ignored this—what must have been a tease, a taunt. "Ryan," she said. "I should go upstairs and get that broom."

He pointed his shard of glass, like a claw, to the clutter beneath the stairs. There were at least three different brooms right there. "Your *r*'s sound great." He rested an elbow on the coffin, which ached under the weight. "And I meant that there are some people you should meet up there for your job.

Casting. I know lots of characters. It'd be like going shopping for people to be in your show or whatever."

"Oh, yes. Well, I really just came to put Caleb on tape."

He stepped toward her. "There we go." He reached out, his hand open in the action grip of a G.I. Joe. His hand was moving toward her face, or her neck, until it wasn't, until it was moving past her, grabbing something on the shelf just behind her. She heard the clink of metal. Something draped lightly across her shoulder as he pulled it toward him.

He held a mess of straps, linked in metal carabiners. In his hands, it was impossible to see the shape of the harness. He began loosening the straps.

"What's that?"

"What I was looking for."

"You found it, then." Bridget again felt that same light-headed wave that the cigarette had given her. It was only in this state—a state that was somehow both pleasant and unpleasant—that she could say, "What is it?"

He looked at her, his lips fixed in a pout of concentration. "Holds the body."

She rubbed her wrists, rotated them freely. "I need to find my associate."

"Needs to bear a lot of resistance." Now he pulled one of the straps through a buckle until it went taut.

"Doesn't need to," she said.

He extended the harness to her. "Want a ride?"

"I just want to find my associate. Please."

"Maybe he'd like a ride? The zip line. Once I get it set up, it'll go from the roof down into our apple orchard. At night, it would be a real rush."

"Oh." She rubbed her wrists again. "No, thank you, Dr. Docter." Saying his name aloud reminded her of a song, dimly recalled, by one of those 60s girl groups, its refrain featuring that one word, chirped twice—"doctor, doctor." Punchy, a trochee, if she correctly remembered those high school poetry lessons. Stress, unstressed.

A cold breeze was coming in through the broken window. He looked to the window, made a small grunt to acknowledge the glass on the floor. "These kids," he said. "Caleb tells 'em about the safe down here and they get aggressive."

"I don't see a safe."

"That's how you keep it safe. My new philosophy is to give them what they want. If kids have booze here, they won't go drinking under an overpass somewhere. But—"

"Don't their parents object?"

"No one objects to the team doctor. Not after we won Nationals."

He was still holding the harness. She touched it, plucked one of the buckles between her fingers. She needed to take charge of this conversation. To push, not pull. "Cheryl never would have let you, right? But after, a perfect way to make the kids happy again."

He gently pulled the harness out of her hand. "No. But why not." The ribbed edges of the strap left a vague sensation of rug burn on her fingers.

She had to recover this. "What about that, the dress form?"

He looked at the dress form. He walked over to it, the grotesque amputee, beheaded in the corner. He stood across from it, less than an arm's length away.

"She sewed? Your wife?" Bridget stepped forward. Now that he'd moved away from the coffin, she could rest her hands on it.

The dress form's dimensions were set small. Cheryl must

have been petite. They were all anorexics, these rich wives, tiny tender creatures with fish bones.

Dr. Docter regarded the dress form where its head would have been, six inches above the stump of its spine, and he said, "No." He lightly touched the bust of the dress form with his thumb. "Got this just for the festivities. Caleb has some plan or another for it."

He wrapped the zip-line harness around the torso of the dress form, took his time getting all the straps arranged correctly. "That's two. You have eighteen left."

"Are we playing twenty questions?" She felt a splinter on the coffin. She pushed her thumb against it, felt its puncture.

"Apparently." He tightened the harness. The dress form wobbled a bit.

"Okay." This felt less like twenty questions, more like an escape room. If she could guess Cheryl's real identity, she'd be let out of the basement. What was Mabel now telling people who asked where her mother had gone? What Bridget-shaped hole would Mabel carve for them with X-Acto precision? "That." She gestured to a saucer sled, red plastic, propped up in the corner. "She liked to sled?"

He didn't take his eyes off the newly strapped dress form. "You're down to seventeen."

She stepped back until something was at her back, the shelf. "The sleeping bags," she said, pointing. "She—liked to sleep? I mean, go camping."

"You're boring me." He began loosening the harness, removing it from the headless woman.

"The stomach, then. What is it?"

The zip-line harness was now loosely draped over the dress form's shoulders. Dr. Docter let go of the straps and the whole thing fell from the shoulders to the floor, looped around the base. He wasn't turning to look at her, or the stomach in the bag. "That wasn't a yes or no question."

"Was she"—of course—"an actress? Was the stomach for a part? She had to play a pregnant woman?"

He finally turned to her, looking at her like she was an inconvenience dimly passing through his day. "You're down to fifteen now."

He walked toward her. The stomach in the bag was just behind her. She moved her right foot back until she felt the bag beneath her heel. He stopped close enough for her to see the quiver of his nose hairs, hear the whistle of each breath's passage. He looked down, just past her, presumably at the bag that bore the rubber pregnant belly. He returned his eyes to hers, perked up his eyebrows. "For Chrissy. If she doesn't take her pill, she has to wear that for a month."

"Why—"

"But I originally got it for her mother."

"Cheryl?"

"She wanted a third. She had to wear that for practice. To remind her—the back pain, you know."

"How'd she do?"

"I broke my own rules."

"What does that mean?"

"I answered something that wasn't a 'yes or no' question."

People were screaming upstairs. Dr. Docter leaned down. He lightly touched her leg in a way that said "move." She stepped aside and he pulled the belly from the bag. It had a real heft to it; she could tell from the way he held it like something once alive.

"You need a costume," he said.

"Oh." She put her hand on her stomach. "I have one. I'm catering." She raised her hands as if to show off her outfit but wound up brushing the rubbery flesh of the belly in his hands. She pulled her hands back to her chest in revulsion.

"We didn't order catering. Lift up your shirt, please."

His voice was firm but soft, a sentence that knew exactly where it was going but was in no rush to get there. This, she supposed, was the vaunted bedside manner. The only doctors she'd been to were either gruff old men whose patience had been worn away or Doogie Howser types who looked like they'd never seen a breast before. Dr. Docter, though, spoke in a way that made her forget she was in a basement toying around with the detritus of a stranger's life.

He did have a point. About the costume. The woman Bertram would recognize was someone who wasn't visibly, undeniably, pregnant. Here was a costume, a cover, an offer of safety.

She lifted the front of her shirt, exposing just her stomach. She inhaled and held it. His fingers were cold. She tensed. "Just relax," he said. "Here. Exposure therapy." He placed his palm flat against her stomach. Her stomach muscles spasmed, and she fought her body to keep still. "You'll get used to it."

She willed herself to stop twitching with discomfort. His hand remained.

That sentence that knew where it was going, it was also spoken with the confidence of knowing it would get there, no matter what. Her hands squeezed the balled-up seams of her shirt.

The path of his thumb on her skin, both dull and sharp, turned an inch into a yard, a second into an hour. She was clenching her teeth.

She heard a light exhalation as he lifted the rubber belly. The rubber was cool against her skin, but it was a dull, diffuse cold, not the icicle-tip of his finger. He reached around to the small of her back and fit the Velcro straps together, snug. He let go and the weight of the rubber belly pulled her center of gravity forward, down.

He touched her hands, pulled the shirt from her grip, and draped her top down over the belly.

He stood back up, faced her. Without looking down, he patted her new fake belly, just as every elderly person in line at the grocery store had patted her real belly, without permission or warning, when she was carrying Jake and Mabel. People became augurs examining the particulars of how she held the weight, or how the weight held her. They examined her, unprompted, like she was a boggy mess of tea leaves at the bottom of a mug. "That's a boy if I ever saw one, trust me." Or: "Two girls, I can tell." Or: "Hysterical pregnancy brought on by economic anxieties." To which she said nothing, just offered a passive smile.

Looking down at this belly that inflated her shirt, she wondered how one might read its contours, the pull of its gravity. She hovered her hand over it, an inch above. "Can I touch it?" she asked, immediately feeling embarrassed.

But the laugh Dr. Docter offered, a faint echo of a laugh from somewhere in the back of his throat, did not seem to be at her expense; it sounded like a genuine response of delight. She saw the way he now looked at her, as if she were actually here; his eyes seemed to focus now. The hollow space of a person he'd been interacting with, she now occupied that space for him. Even if he knew all about her, even if he saw through the machinations of her plans, he now seemed activated by the fiction she was offering. He could not have cared less for the possibilities her initial premise had offered—the money and fame of a child going off to Hollywood—but here, this was something.

She put her hand on the upper hemisphere of the belly, of her belly. It wasn't her skin, wasn't her body, but she felt something, a mere suggestion, a phantom touch. She slid her hand down, then back up. Rubbing it was nice, comforting.

"How's that feel?" he asked.

"Familiar," she said.

"So this isn't your first?"

Her mouth was dry. Swallowing only made her want to cough. "I have a son."

"Vaginal or C-section?"

She felt a pang of guilt for having excluded Mabel. "And a daughter." Even though this was just a scene, a fiction in which anyone could be anything. "They were twins."

He touched the belly on the bottom, right where it sloped into her. He moved his hand further, to where rubber met skin.

"Still are," she said. "Twins, I mean."

"C-section," he said.

"The doctor said I had to."

"That right?"

"He said I couldn't accommodate them." That word, accommodate, had surprised her, the ease of its sound, the stairstep of syllables.

"That's what I tell relatives I don't want visiting."

She surprised herself with a tiny burst of a laugh.

"Well," he continued, "your womb isn't a guest room with a foldout. It's your body, and it's my job to help your body accommodate."

She tried to make her sigh of relief and gratitude seem in-character, not genuine.

"But," he said, "if you're hoping for a vaginal delivery after the C-section, it won't be easy."

"I know."

"It can be dangerous."

She rubbed her belly. Her fingers lingered on the distended belly button. "I know."

"We should make sure the baby is positioned correctly." He put his right hand on her arm and gestured with his left hand toward the trifold futon on the floor. Bridget's college roommate had a name for that kind of futon.

She said, "On the flip-and-fuck?"

Dr. Docter was unfazed. "Please."

She walked over. The weight of the belly made her waddle, her lower back pulled forward. She reached for his hand to steady herself as she lowered her body to the futon on the floor. She leaned back and—the new addition to her body forced her to—put her weight on her hands behind her, her legs splayed out. He kneeled on the floor, positioned himself in front of her.

He placed a hand on her knee.

Upstairs, the bass from the stereo sounded like an off-balance washing machine.

She lifted her foot. Dr. Docter's hand slid from her knee. She placed her foot on his chest.

He put his hand around her ankle.

She pushed.

He squeezed.

This was when someone would say, "Scene," and their characters would vaporize. Instead, she said, "You need gloves."

He scrunched his nose in something adjacent to a smile. "No, I don't."

"Yes. You do."

"I need to feel what I'm touching."

She'd done her part, done enough to gain some leverage. She pushed her foot harder against his chest. She said, "There's a box of gloves upstairs, in the kitchen."

He held his breath, then exhaled. He loosened his grip on her ankle. "Wait here."

When the popular film critic inevitably invited her back to the house—that he said was not his but that he stayed in because its owner, a different professor famous for his cultural history of mummification, spent semesters in Istanbul aligned with the popular film critic's semesters here—she said yes because she really needed to pee and her apartment was on the other side of campus. As she pissed in the popular film critic's borrowed bathroom, she listened to him prepare another drink in the living room, knowing that if she could hear him that meant that he could hear her, the tiled walls surely amplifying the trill of her pee. When she came back out, she was anticipating his advances, though unsure how exactly she would respond. But things did not progress as she'd expected. He asked her if she'd sit down beside him, and she did, and he explained that at this point in his life the greatest pleasure was just being in proximity to someone as youthful and lovely as she. Okay. He said her youth made him feel so old, but no, not in a bad way, in a nice way, you see. She didn't see. Sometimes, he said, he thought how nice it would be when he was really old and bedridden and had to be taken care of by someone so young and lovely, and she wouldn't even know he was there, and just think of the eroticism of that, the unreciprocated knowledge of the other. Uh-huh. And one day, he explained, he'd be lying dead somewhere, in a hospital or morgue, and someone like her, young and lovely, would be there, working, cleaning up or preparing or not doing anything at all. Like this, he said, and he closed his eyes and he leaned back on the couch. She could see him relax, not just ease into a reclining position but really relax, like something load-bearing had slipped from his body.

And he stayed like that, not trying to kiss her or touch her, just pretending to be dead, while she sat beside him. She wasn't sure if what he was getting from this little exercise—which was stretching into ten, fifteen minutes, more—was meditative or erotic, but she felt something surprising in the audience she kept over his performative corpse: She felt an alarming power. She could hurt him, rob him, do anything. The minutes kept going by until they became meaningless; the only unit of time was the unit of thought she used to decide to *not* do something. So, as the night crept on, she sat in that knowledge, held it like a secret, potent.

● **REC**

A screen gone blue, the blue of blue sky, open and vast, but also a blue that is closed, a blue of not seeing, a blue of technical difficulties—until it blinks and a torso fills the frame, a torso covered in a shirt that a voice is chanting for the removal of. The wearer of the shirt declines and her hand soon fills the frame, grabs it, a lifeline suddenly in focus.

13.

After Dr. Docter had walked back upstairs, out of the basement, Bridget remained supine on the flip-and-fuck. Above her, the ceiling displayed water stains like the maps inside the flyleaves of the fantasy books Jake used to read, or just look at.

When she was a kid, she'd read stories about spontaneous quadriplegia, people waking up and no longer able to move. She went through months, years of waking up and wondering if in the night she'd been mysteriously afflicted, knowing that the only way to find out was to attempt movement. Until she tried to move—to twitch her finger, shift her leg, raise her head—the possibility of her spinal and neurological integrity remained intact, but so did the possibility of those systems' complete collapse.

The closest she got to paralysis came after she gave birth to Jake and Mabel. In the ICU, she examined the pocked texture of ceiling tile and felt only the rising panic when she realized she couldn't move her legs. It was the same sensation she'd had before the C-section, but that had been different: Then, she'd been part of something, her body conscripted to a project beyond herself. Now, the little bodies she'd made had been taken away, whisked off to the NICU, and she was left alone with a body that was no longer responding to her requests, a body that was deciding to ignore her. There, she found none of the comfort, and could access none of the coping skills that she'd been so focused on developing, back in the imagined paralysis of her youth. She felt only the slow dripping leak of dread.

Now, in Dr. Docter's basement, she pulled herself to her knees, then her feet.

The safe. This junk room of a basement, like a net that caught all the detritus of domestic life, was as good a place as any to stash such a thing. But even if she found it, what would she do with it? Safecracking was not in her skillset. Still, Bridget could just as easily picture the safe unlocked. A wealth like the Docters' was arrogant enough to behave recklessly. That, after all, was the tenet underpinning her and Jake's entire con. She had to find it.

With the fake pregnant belly strapped to her, she waddled over to a metal shelf on which sat clear plastic garbage bags filled with dolls and stuffed animals. Their faces were smooshed up against the plastic, three-dimensional faces distorted into two, features crowding into the same plane. She poked the face of a bear, imagined its fluffy body filled with the cache of Docter cash. Perhaps if she ran a knife up the belly of Paddington, he'd sprout greenbacks.

Between two shelves, a few framed paintings were propped up and draped with a baby blanket. The baby blanket seemed like it had once been yellow. The paintings, from the corners she could obliquely see, were shit-tone landscapes, motel-quality paintings. Surely she'd seen some movie where valuables were hidden in the pulled canvas of paintings like these. She didn't bother.

These were not the details that illuminated a life. These were the details that asphyxiated life with banalities.

But here: on the bottom of the adjacent shelf, a photo

album. Its cover was plaid cloth. She picked it up. It crinkled in her hands. The first page featured baby pictures from the early 80s with a color palette that seemed like they'd been processed in coffee and ketchup. Parents in poofy hair, feathered and unfortunate. On the next page, the kids got older, pawed at gifts under a Christmas tree. A woman's acrylic nails reached into frame.

A few pages on, after Caleb and Chrissy had begun to emerge as children recognizable from their adolescent futures, the pictures began to lose their crisp, clean edges. And they began to feature one person only: a woman, presumably their mother. Here was a photo of her that had clearly been cut out of a larger family photo, her putting her arm around someone unseen, their body cut off by a crisp edge. There were more, some of her X-Acto-knifed out of the middle of pictures, some neatly removed from the side. This was a photo album of exile, the space to which this woman had been banished, having clearly been cast out of the complete family photos, presumably kept elsewhere, safe from whatever harm her very image was imagined to cause.

The woman's smiling face was oblivious. Bridget hated this woman, for smiling, for not seeing what was coming.

Bridget had always known what was coming, even if she couldn't see it. She had always known that Mabel would be able to see something wrong in her. She just didn't realize that what Mabel saw were the shameful facts of fraud encrypted in IRS notices and credit card statements as if in a Mayan codex. It was never a question of if, but of when and how. The whens, the hows—being a parent meant the children scattered the whens and hows of your doom, like tiny toys lost in couch cushions; she knew they were there, somewhere. And so when the G-men came in the form of her own daughter, Mabel handing her findings over to Tod, Bridget at least felt something akin to relief: *Oh, there it is.* That attitude, though, that fatalist sense of passive inevitability, did her no good. That was the Bridget who almost drove away, leaving Jake behind. That was the Bridget who would rather crumple into a ball in a darkened vanity closet than do what she needed to, which was simple: Anticipate it, stay ahead of it, just like the advice for taking painkillers, know that the pain is lurking out there and go find it.

She closed the album. She placed it back on the shelf.

Bridget tumbled her body back onto the flip-and-fuck. She cradled her belly. Everything ached and her hands stayed still when palming the rubber elasticity of her prosthetic pregnancy.

She felt something poking her thigh. She reached into her pocket and pulled out the pink eyebrow tweezers from the Foothill Square Mall. She dropped them to the floor beside the futon.

She needed to find her son. She needed to get out of here, abandon all hope of a score—and its attendant promise of escape from the tether to Tod—and just get out, get safe. Marks weren't supposed to come back. But she also needed to lie here—for just one more second—and cradle a rubber belly strapped to her body as if it were really gestating something new, someone new. She pressed her palm into her new belly, imagined searching for the kicks and turns of personhood. What was the opposite of a hysterical pregnancy? Not the sensation of something real that turns out to be illusory, but the initial illusion becoming real? A rational pregnancy?

No, what was rational was getting up off her ass. What was rational was keeping this belly on, staying disguised from Bertram. What was rational was getting Jake and getting out of here. Besides, if this job didn't work, that meant he'd stay with her. At least that's what he'd said; that was the deal. He'd promised.

Upstairs, footsteps moved in patterns like flocks of birds, gathering in swirls, then dispersing out in ellipses again. One set moved in a straight line, a line that led right to the sound of the basement door opening, a spasm of noise and music dilating until that door closed again. Those footsteps became suddenly and crisply audible, descending the unfinished wooden stairs. Then the granular scrape of shoes moved across not lumber but cement.

A hand on her shoulder, the astringent scent of latex. "Wakey, wakey."

She felt in her new belly something faint, subcutaneous, submuscular, a movement. She pressed.

Dr. Docter began rubbing her back, pressing the heel of his hand against the muscles clinging to her scapula. "Am I gonna have to get the smelling salts?"

Her hand met resistance, a shape she tried to find the contours of. Pressing into her belly like this, it was quite uncomfortable, but between her own probings and Dr. Docter's, she was a science experiment on the petri dish of the flip-and-fuck futon.

Dr. Docter's hand moved to her bare neck, his latex on the skin of her nape. His hands didn't quite grip the muscles of her neck, though they did toggle her vertebrae like they were beads on an abacus. A crinkling pain emerged.

"Or stay asleep," he said. "I don't really mind."

She turned, rolled onto her back, her eyes now open. Her movement forced his hand from her neck. Dr. Docter, kneeling beside her, his face looming above her, said, "Hello, there."

She had a spelunker's view into his nostrils.

"Let's see how the baby's doing," he said, putting his hand at the bottom of her belly. Then he inched his hand down.

"Last time," she said, "it was a mess."

"We should get you out of these pants."

"They had to cut me open."

"Now, my hands might be a little cold, but—"

She grabbed his wrists. "Stop."

He twisted in her grasp.

"Don't." She twisted his wrists and turned to get her leg between them, her knee to his chest.

His weight was on her. She pushed her knee against his solar plexus.

Her right hand braced against the floor, her thumb felt a poke. Her fingers wrapped around the tweezers.

She brought the tweezers around in a jab.

He let out a little sound that was part cough and part grunt.

She had no idea what part of his body she'd made contact with, but he was easier to push away with her leg now. He stumbled onto his ass, his right hand holding the left side of his abdomen.

She pushed herself up to her knees and made sure the belly was still secured. The straps were a bit twisted, but the Velcro had held.

"Damnit," Dr. Docter said.

"Did I stab you?" She felt momentarily safe, then panic, previously held at bay, flooded in. "Are you hurt?"

He took his hand from his wound, inspected his fingers. "I think I'll need some Neosporin." She couldn't see blood on his hands, though he was looking at something, maybe a drop or two. He asked, "Was that your fingernail? Or your ring?"

She looked at her engagement ring. "I should stop wearing this."

"You don't need to stop wearing it, just stop poking people with it." He was rubbing his side. "Why'd you do that?"

"I'm sorry."

"Christ, I thought we were, like, doing a thing."

She rubbed the stomach, her stomach, reclaimed and saved from threat, felt her fingers over the distended belly button. Her eyes went to the threadwork of her shirt, a moth-eaten hole. She fingered the hole, felt the rubber of the belly beneath, pressed it until the material no longer felt alien.

The sound of him stomping off through the outside door was the sound of the window glass crunching underfoot, then the light crepitation of feet on the grass just outside.

She waited. She wasn't going to open her eyes until she was positive they wouldn't see him. Or anyone. She closed her eyes so tight phosphenes swelled in bursts, kaleidoscopic concussions of color just for her.

She opened her eyes. The visual world of demonstrably real objects returned, the world you had to share with others, bouncing light into her eyes, and this world scattered away the smears and swirls that had been there a moment ago.

The basement was empty. The door was open. It was cold. She was free to find her son. She kept a hand on her belly.

When she'd first told people she was having twins, it felt like she was telling them she was entering into the world of the Brothers Grimm. People came at her with any scrap of folklore they had stashed in the crannies of their brains, ideas about the dark and unexplained possibilities that twins foretold. The twins would invent their own language. They would develop complex forms of prelingual communication while in the womb. The twins would be indistinguishable even to their parents and so what even was identity? There was something about the doubling of twins that turned everyone witchy. Much of this augury was easy for Bridget to dismiss, except for one thing that her hair stylist told her, as she sat trapped in her chair, staring at her own face. (There was a social power dynamic wielded by stylists that too many of them abused, the way, with scissors hovering around your face, they could steer conversations anywhere they desired.) The stylist told her she had heard of something called vanishing twin syndrome, where you'd like see two babies in the ultrasound but then you'd go back for another ultrasound later and there'd only be one baby, and the one had like absorbed the other, like it had eaten it.

The antiseptic smell of that salon was what she anticipated the hospital would smell like, but it didn't. And every time she went in for another ultrasound there would be a moment when only one twin was visible, and in the moment it took the technician to locate the second one, Bridget's heart both seized and settled into a knowledge, a knowledge that seemed inevitable, that her body was the site of a violence so primal it could not be seen or acknowledged. She'd never mention this concern to a doctor, much less Tod; the fear of uttering it was too bound up in the act that it signified.

When she ate, when she felt an overwhelming appetite, part of her imagined that this was a demand that if unmet would result in what, in her mind, had taken on the specter of a prophecy. Eating was an act of placating something, appeasing something with awful potential. Her reference points for changes in mood, in desires, were no longer the dogeared manuals that stacked up on Tod's side of the bed, but rather the same bits of partially imagined and partially remembered folklore that turned fears into fate.

In the end, when there were two, she still couldn't hold off the intrusive thoughts that demanded to know which body would have absorbed the other. She knew that weaning went both ways, that just as infants needed to realize they were separate bodies from the mother, so too the mother came to realize she was a separate body from the infants, but this struck her as placing too much faith in the impermeability of the body. The skin, the pore, it breathed, it consumed, it ate. Which side of the ravenous membrane you were on was not always clear, or important.

But soon she found something new, something worse: an understanding that it wasn't a fear of the devouring child but a fear of the unsustaining mother. The body unaccommodating. In that first year of parenthood, she would refrain from mentioning any of this to those who tried to untangle whatever sense of doom kept her bedridden and despondent.

But she'd done it. She'd sustained them both. There, Jake. There, Mabel. Two separate squishy things, clearly identifiable and not conspiring with each other in some Klingon-sounding argot. She'd sustained them both, until she hadn't. Until the older (by three minutes, three minutes that seemed to dilate into years) discovered just some of the ways her mother was a fraud, undeserving of home and kin. And then there was only one, one she could sustain, sustain by hook or by crook, only one she could guide through life unharmed. Until even he wanted to flee from her, run back to the accommodating home.

There, in the basement of Dr. Docter's house, she got to her feet. She considered escaping through the outside door, but no. Dr. Docter had gone that way. And her son was upstairs, somewhere up in the rest of the house where music was rending the air like brain damage.

She went to the stairs that led up to the rest of the house. The soles of her shoes on the wooden stairs sounded like hooves on cobblestones. As she approached the top, the music became less something she heard, more something she felt. It vibrated her diaphragm. At the top of the stairs, she put her hand on the doorknob. As she held it, it turned, but she had not turned it. Someone on the other side of the door had their hand on the doorknob and was opening the door. The music entered like a miasma. The door opened a crack, then stopped. She moved back down two steps, as quietly as she could. Through the hand-size crack in the door, a figure, his face turned away from the basement, was yelling back at someone: "Just tell Ethan to come help me in the basement!" Behind him, people were screaming. He continued: "Fine, I'll get him." And, leaving the door ajar, he walked away, back into the house.

Bridget hurried down the stairs, her feet sliding from step to step. Her descent down the stairs was more a controlled fall, but she stuck the landing at the bottom and in a few strides was at the outside door. But there she stopped still. A shadowy band of teenagers was approaching from the backyard. Above her, the door opened again, letting two voices into the basement: from the sounds of it, the kid who'd been demanding help from Ethan, and, with him, Ethan.

Her eyes alighted on the only option. She moved swiftly to the coffin, opened its lid—the ghoulish thing was blessedly empty—and she crawled in, closing the lid above her just as those voices descended.

● **REC**

The frame is dark but soon illuminated by a source just out of frame, a flashlight perhaps. The frame follows that searching beam of light as if there's been a prison break. That little spotlight points urgently at the sneakered feet of passersby, then suddenly up to their faces, hands grasping defensively at the glare.

14.

The coffin was sealed black. Bridget waited for her eyes to adjust. They did not adjust.

And what, she suddenly wondered, had Jake said to his father, on the phone at the motel?

Outside, the voices—dimmed through cheap lumber—cackled. The two boys, Ethan and someone else, teased each other in ways she could only recognize by inflection. They weren't saying much in the way of words, but there was the punctuation of movement that suggested roughhousing. Although when boys their age did it, it wasn't roughhousing; it was just violence.

Her eyes were still not detecting a hint of light. When her eyes were open, they strained to look so hard into the unrelenting darkness of the coffin. She had to close her eyes, trading one darkness for another, just to force her eyes to stop trying to find the light that wasn't there.

And who, she suddenly wondered, had initiated that conversation, that conversation about Jake coming home, on the phone at the motel—Jake or Tod?

The wood of the coffin was splintery and flaky. It was particle board. Her fingers found scabs of wood, peeled them free. She rotated one in her fingers, thin as skin.

Her hair was catching in the creases of the particle board. Any movement of her head, no matter how careful, tugged at a few strands. Little pings of pain constellated her scalp.

Suddenly a smack came down on the top of the coffin, an impact inches from her face. Her body convulsed in alarm, and she clutched her belly, stabilizing herself.

That one thump was followed by a series of rapid drumrolls, then Ethan's voice: "Get that end."

"I got a splinter!"

"Jesus Christ, seriously?"

The whole coffin jostled, and Bridget held her breath—or she didn't so much hold it as grab it, wrestle it under control. She clenched her jaw.

When the coffin was lifted, she held the inside walls to keep from bumping around. Her arms were taut with exertion. Her feet and knees likewise pressed against the wood. Her whole body flexing out as this thing was now levitating.

Outside, the two boys continued berating each other's pain tolerance, such insults focusing on splinters, how many splinters each could handle.

"You go up first," Ethan said.

"No."

"You're already at the stairs, just walk up."

"Backwards! That means I have to be the one to walk up backwards. *You* walk up backwards."

"I'm helping *you* out!"

The non-Ethan kid let out a groan—his voice constricted by the effort of holding the coffin—and she heard his foot hit the first step.

"Pivot!"

Step by step, the bottom end of the coffin began ratcheting up, and her head started to get pulled back. As they began carrying this thing up the stairs, she had to tap every reservoir of strength to keep her body from sliding back. If there was anything suspicious, or even curious, about the weight distribution in this coffin, they'd surely open it up, only for Ethan to find the woman who'd just scammed his parents out of thousands of dollars, the woman who would then be captive in a plywood box.

The drunken pallbearers breathed in curses.

Her own breath needed escape, but it was so pressurized by now that she couldn't just let it out. She had to exert just as much energy to ease it out, then exchange that breath for something new to hold captive in her chest.

Her vanity room in her old house in Denver had likely been repainted. By now, Tod had discovered the hole behind that one octagonal mirror, the hole in which she'd stored her cache of pre-approveds. Her hands now touched no such reserves. These walls were devastatingly bare, flat and absolute.

The drunken pallbearers leveled out her coffin. They must have been upstairs now. The music surrounded her, closed in. It filled the coffin like water, her lungs constricting.

A jolt, an impact: the force almost snapping back her fingers, spidered out against the wood. They must have bashed into a corner because the not-Ethan again shouted, "Pivot!"

Tod had once told her that locked in her vanity room she was a little pearl, that she'd go into it an irritant and be smoothed over—with foundation, mascara and eyeliner—until she emerged an object of beauty: to which she'd said, or rather thought, Fuck you. But now, locked in this casket, she was the inverse: She'd entered this enclosure as something resembling a presentable human and she was now being refined down to her original form as an irritant.

The drunken pallbearers were setting the coffin down now,

the clump of the coffin getting settled onto something blessedly stable.

It was strange, she'd thought, that an oyster's response to an irritant was generative—here was a new thing, made from both, the synthesis almost procreative, hereditary—while most organisms she knew simply expelled the offending thing.

Above her, a foot or two away from her face, mediated only by black-painted particle board, Ethan said, "Splinters in my hands."

She kept her hands and feet braced against the interior walls, though she wasn't sure if that was her choice or her body's.

"Seriously," the other kid said, "what's even in this thing?"

She wasn't sure if she'd closed her eyes or her eyes were already closed, but she clenched her entire face as if she could pull her whole body into a single point and—like an iris closing in a final fade-out—disappear.

"Dummy, I think," Ethan said. "Caleb said they got the CPR dummies from the pool."

They would look in the coffin. They would find her. She'd play dead, or play dummy. She opened her mouth in the open scream of a CPR dummy.

"Why's the pool have dummies?"

"Lifeguard training, idiot."

"Don't call me an idiot!"

Then: the arrhythmic punctuations of teenage violence, and soon enough, instead of investigating the contents of the coffin, the two seemed to leave the room—and it did sound like she had been left in a room, the way a closing door once again dimmed the music.

She waited, willed her hands and feet to relax, against their better judgment.

Her hands found comfort and purpose on her belly.

She desperately wanted to burst out of this thing—the vanity it wasn't; she did not control the particulars of this containment, this darkness—but she knew she had to wait, give it time until it was safe.

She tried to remember some song to sing silently to herself to mark the passage of time, time being the first thing to turn hallucinogenic when in total darkness, not space, but she could only come up with the kind of kid jingles that she'd sung to Jake and Mabel when they were babies, songs that had been sung to her when she was a baby, songs that only when she sang them did she recognize their utter insanity, as so many of the lyrics were formed around idiomatic expressions and cryptic Old-World allusions that made them both folksy and, when you found those words coming out of your own mouth, terrifying, an incantatory menace. She still had no clue what it really meant to "ride a cock-horse to Banbury Cross, / to see a fine lady upon a white horse." There was something dimly Masonic or even druidic in its iconography, images that were now in Jake and Mabel's heads to pass on, a generational refrain.

A few weeks after her first encounter with the popular film critic's interest in playacting a corpse for her disinterested audience, he asked her to stay behind after class. They'd just watched a segment of *Roman Holiday*—slowed, distorted, reversed and contorted before their eyes—in which Audrey Hepburn steered a Vespa lunatically around the city, Gregory Peck sitting behind her, and the popular film critic had observed that this display of vehicular strength turned broken and comic was anti-Futurism, but now with the rest of the students safely out of earshot he said he had a surprise to show her. For some reason, she imagined this surprise to be a rare print of some film, the possibilities of which she ran through in her head as the two of them walked back to his temporary home, and all the while he was reeling off his bizarre knowledge of her negligible little acting career, guiding her through the quad like a tour guide to her own life.

When they got back to the modestly sized craftsman, which he said was just outside the radius in which one might have to deal with the errant undergrad puking on the lawn ("The Dean," he said, "lives just a block closer to the library and regularly wakes up to find football players passed out on her couch, having mistaken her house for their frat house"), he showed her, draped over a chair in his living room, a large black vinyl bag. He presented it to her as if it were the Emmy he'd earlier insisted *In a Pickle* should have received (it deserved no such thing). What, she wanted to know, was it? Why, a body bag, of course. Yes, of course. Look, he said, and he unzipped it and displayed for her the inside, which was just like the outside only it was on the inside. The zipper tab, he pointed out, was only on the outside. Wasn't that interesting? But what if, she asked, someone was placed in there by mistake? They'd be unable to free themselves. Ah, good point. But that, he explained, was why—though not the only reason—he had invited her to see this. The not having a zipper tag on the inside meant that he was unable to completely zip this up from the inside. Would she do the honors?

After clearing a few stacks of books, he got down on the floor and folded himself in as if into a sleeping bag. He gestured for her to zip him up. She leaned down, seeing that he was already closing his eyes and relaxing into his imagined death, and she zipped the bag up, the zipper's teeth closing over his serene face. While he remained there on the floor, she took the opportunity to do some reading—not for his class (he didn't assign any reading), but for her anthro class—as she'd brought her backpack. *Tristes Tropiques* made for oddly agreeable company in the tranquil morgue of this borrowed home. When she took a break and walked across the living room toward the bathroom, she accidentally kicked his body. Oh, God, sorry, she said. He didn't make a noise, just a little puff of breath under the vinyl. She watched him for a moment, amazed that the accidental shoe-tip to the head didn't break his performance. As she was watching him, she noticed a slight elevation in the vinyl at waist-level. She could hear his breath, rapid. She placed the tip of her foot lightly on the bag about where his chest seemed to be. She pressed down, slowly, as if on a gas pedal. She could hear the bellows of his lungs deflate a little under her shoe, this time with a guttural note of pleasure, a purr. She removed her foot from his body. She stood back. Then she began kicking.

She now pushed open the lid of her coffin. A blade of light entered. As she kept pushing the lid farther open, she expected that blade of light to expand. But it didn't. The source was a single bulb from a string of Christmas lights hanging on the ceiling. All but one of the little bulbs were either extinguished or absent from the strand. The rest of the room was unlit, though she was surprised by how much detail that tiny little light was able to reveal. It had a moonlight effect on the room, and she soon realized this was intentional.

Sitting up in the coffin, which was lying flat on a wobbly table, she saw she was in a small room decorated as a midnight cemetery. The walls had a texture to them that created the effect of staring into dark woods, an effect created—her eyes adjusting—by black burlap hung from the ceiling, draped in irregular pleats. On the floor around her, tombstones emerged from a floor covered in something resembling foliage.

She crawled out of the coffin, carefully. Putting her foot over the edge and onto the table proved more precarious than she expected. She was worried that she'd topple the whole thing over, but she managed to get out of the coffin and onto the floor. Crouching now in the ersatz cemetery, she realized her belly might have aided in her balance, the strange magic it did to her center of gravity. The material that lined the floor and gave it the look and texture of an overgrown graveyard seemed to be old fur coats, cut up and pieced together.

Beside her ,one of the interred corpses had begun to rise from its rest. A single arm emerged, radius and ulna exposed, flesh torn away but still clinging in chunks. Beside it, a skull wore, incongruously, a wig. Though color was dimmed to nearly a grayscale in this room, the wig appeared to be purple.

She grabbed the wig, flipped it onto her head, then stood up and saw herself in the sliver of an exposed windowpane, a rending in the fabric of the illusion. If costume was character, performance power, then what was she?

Coffin Momma.

The door rattled. Someone fumbled with the doorknob.

Bridget vaulted herself back into the coffin and pulled the lid down—gently, quietly—just as she heard the door open and two more idiots enter.

The wig smelled like the green plastic grass of a child's Easter basket. It had the texture of floss.

The commentary of the two visitors outside her coffin was mostly, drunkenly, an arrangement of vowels demonstrating awe.

Beyond those sounds, the music was remixing familiar Halloween ditties—goofily affected voices warbling about a "Monster Mash" and a "Purple People Eater"—filtered through some sort of industrial paroxysm, a sonic effect of something simple being broken, being sawed with rusted, serrated blades. No note was safe: anything could suddenly be stretched, distorted, spun out into a droning anti-note.

"Are we supposed to open this?" It was the voice of a young woman.

A tap-tapping on the lid of Bridget's coffin.

She instantly pulled her wig down to cover her face, forced her body to go—or appear—slack, affecting the unnatural posture of a plastic dummy.

She heard the lid open above her.

"Ohhh, fuck." It was the voice of a young man.

"Oh, my God."

"They got a pregnant one?"

"Babe, you don't have to cover your nose. It doesn't smell. It's not real."

"No, I think there is a smell. I think they like sprayed it with corpse smell. Or they like hid a rotten piece of cheese somewhere in there, for realism. You don't smell that?"

"I can't believe they made it pregnant. Caleb is so messed up."

"I bet it was Chrissy's idea. She went to that Hell House in Battenville."

"Is Chrissy like that?"

"I think she was just, like, gathering ideas. Saw all that abortion stuff, gay dudes burning."

"Are they gonna have an abortion room?" the young woman said. "I'm not seeing that stuff."

"This dummy looks so real."

"Don't!"

Bridget could feel a flutter of hands above her.

"What?"

"You can't touch it!"

"Why? It's not a museum."

"Isn't it?"

"You can touch anything in a haunted house."

"Since when?"

"Since now."

Bridget felt a poke on her belly and that poke instantly launched her right foot into the air—as if it were a simple reflex, a button releasing a spring-released kick, a kick that connected her foot with something solid but crunchy in the way that only a face can be.

Sitting up, parting the plastic hair from her face, she saw a young man scrambling backward, clutching his bloodied face. She heard screaming. The young woman was both trying to tend to her partner and cowering in fear at the sight of a resurrected woman.

"She's alive!" the young man said, his vowels bubbling with blood. He spit red onto the young woman's face. Some got into her eye, and she turned down to wipe her eyes clear. When she looked back up, her eyes, cheeks, forehead, and the bridge of her nose were smeared red.

Bridget was out of the coffin now, standing above them.

The young woman shouted at the young man, "I told you not to touch it!"

To Bridget, he screamed, "Don't kill us!"

It had not occurred to Bridget to do so. But she *was* in a position to do great violence to this person. She already had.

The young woman gently helped him pull his hand from his face and what was underneath was the mess of a nose, a bridge of exposed bone.

She looked at her shoes, uncertain how they had the severity of material to scrape the flesh from this poor kid's face. It must have been the velocity. Hers.

Maybe it wasn't quite his bone that had been exposed. The fleck of white she'd seen now seemed to be a curl of skin hanging off. Still—

They continued screaming, apparently unsure if they should be tending to his injury or bracing for more or—the young woman now reaching for whatever her hand could grasp—retaliate. Her hand found the skeleton arm emerging from the grave. She yanked it free and threw it at Bridget. Bridget deflected, swatting away the bony forearm. This, the flailing of her arms, must have looked to the young man like Bridget was lashing out again, because he spasmed in fright and kicked impotently at Bridget's ankles. The young woman was reaching for another weapon, something sturdier—the leg of the table. Her hand wrapped around it and she pulled, her eyes still on Bridget. The table wobbled just enough for the coffin to come sliding off, the side hitting Bridget in the back of her knees. Her legs buckled. She collapsed to the floor, the coffin pinning her legs down at the knees. The pain in her legs was dull but twisting.

The woman was helping the man to his feet. She'd balled up some unidentifiable bit of clothing to staunch the blood. They were trying to make it to the door but that meant making it by Bridget. Their feet were within grabbing distance. They knew it. Bridget could tell from their skittish little steps.

"No trouble," the woman was saying, "no trouble."

Through purple glossy strands, Bridget saw them moving past her, then away from her. They were almost to the door, too nervous to take their eyes off her.

"Wait," Bridget said.

For some reason, they did.

"Help?"

The young man and the young woman looked at each other, gauging the other's interest in this proposition. The young man's breathing—through broken bone, sinuses clotted with blood, and a stray sock shoved against his nostrils—was audible even over the music from the other room.

Again Bridget said, "Help?"

The young woman looked at the coffin pinning Bridget to the floor by the back of her knees. She finally said, "I'm sorry."

The young woman opened the door and ushered the bleeding man out.

Outside the door, it—a room or hallway, she couldn't tell—was draped in black but flared like aurora borealis with ribbons of blue and green neon. As the door was closing, she caught a glimpse of a figure, a figure passing obliquely away, a figure half obscured by wall and door, a figure slouching at just the right cowering angle to be: Jake.

And then the door was closed again. And she was alone. And pinned down by her own coffin. And she hadn't even had the wherewithal or the breath to shout his name.

Now she started screaming.

● **REC**

That voice urges others to undress, is unsuccessful. Soon you are following the backs of two people, one clothed black, the other white. A flurry of dark arms garland the frame, ophidian and emphatic. The figure in white, wearing the black bowler hat, opens a door as if calling it into existence, and through it you follow the two into an empyrean invitation of light.

15.

The screaming worked. It seemed to marshal reserves of strength. She pushed herself up and the coffin fell to the side. It landed on her right pinkie finger. An alarm blared below her fingernail, and she clenched her teeth and turned on her back and kicked the coffin. Then she kept kicking it until it gave in, the particle board revealing fibers and chips. The side wall of the coffin didn't break in a single crack, but rather became soft, weakened.

She got to her feet and sucked her pinkie finger. The nail was warmer than it should be. She took it out of her mouth and tried to look at it, but it was too dark to see the damage. For some reason, without the visual confirmation of injury, she was able to convince herself that it didn't exist, that those signals running up her arm and into her parietal lobe were imaginary.

She balled her hand into a fist and went to the door. She had to find Jake.

If Dr. Docter found him first, then who knows what he'd do: call authorities whose belts were weighted with more than just stun guns, authorities who'd detain him for details of their crimes? But Dr. Docter didn't seem the type to defer to others.

He seemed like a man who'd prefer DIY justice, retribution. Jake didn't have money, didn't have access to it, didn't have the coping skills to navigate any kind of confrontation like that. She'd felt the doctor's hands, knew the force of his grip.

She clutched the doorknob, yanked the door open. No light flooded in. But the darkness of the hallway was not static. It moved in gyrations, throbbed and flailed. She inhaled, held it, and walked into the hall.

The trick was simple and terrifying: The walls were draped with black sheets. People were hiding behind the sheets, their arms—in black sleeves and black gloves—emerging from tears and grabbing anything and anyone. The hallway was completely tentacled with grasping arms. She ran down the hall in the direction she thought she saw Jake go.

She didn't get two steps before the hands got her. While most of the hands grasped impotently at her, one wrapped itself firmly around her arm, just above the elbow. When she tried to twist away and peel the fingers off, another one, from the opposite side of the hallway, got her by the wrist.

The hands were as multitudinous as bees in a swarm. Writhing away, she ducked down and fought on—though she saw no light, just a dark throb, a birth canal with no exit—and, despite her low crouch, hands seemed to be grasping down at her face now, fingers poking into her eyes like her skull was a bowling ball. Bruise-colored circles bloomed within circles beneath her eyelids.

Or, worse than the vengeful clutch of the doctor, a menacing thought: Would Jake manifest as one of the countless bodies that had been absorbed into this haunted house? Was this his arm, his hand? If not his, then whose? The rapacity with which these hands pulled at her suggested something more than mere fun, or something that had pierced the membrane of fun, found the malice beneath. Whatever had compelled all these bodies into choreographed mania could surely have seduced Jake. After all, he had built up zero tolerance to peer pressure. Did that make *him* the perfect mark? What if she never found him? What if he'd found his new home?

Another hand was pawing at her belly. She started kicking at it. It tried to defensively grasp at her ankle but stopped when she felt something snap beneath her kick—the break of an index finger, she assumed, hoped.

The yelp of pain told her this wasn't Jake.

She saw something ahead, a glint of something: metal reflecting a blue-green light that undulated above. This was a doorknob, maybe just a few feet away. She pushed her way toward it and grabbed hold.

The door opened inward and as she pulled herself through it, into a blinding white light, she kept one hand over her belly and kicked back at the black-draped walls.

Nearly two decades ago, she'd go to the popular film critic's borrowed home once a week and kick the shit out of him. Often he'd already be in his body bag when she arrived, which made her uncomfortable and a little angry, as he'd first asked for her assistance in zipping it all the way up, which he said he couldn't do by himself from the inside, and now clearly he was able to do that. If he'd just been lying to her about zipping it up, then it felt like a betrayal, though if he'd since learned how to zip himself up, then good for him.

Sometimes there would be a note on top of the body bag and on the note, handwritten requests for treatments that Bridget did not provide the entombed man, preferring instead the kind of mid-torso kicking that she'd first felt inspired to, though sometimes she kicked by not kicking, the withholding its own kind of violence. She did enjoy seeing him visibly achy around the midsection in class, mumbling something about pulling a muscle. In the years after this relationship, as she would come to categorize it—those afternoons sitting in that living room with a make-believe corpse on the floor, a thick course reader open on her lap, the afternoon light coming in canted, the tang of lemon-scented polish clinging to the many wooden surfaces—Bridget would consider these the most peaceful and domestic moments of her life.

Here was a room with white walls reflecting more light than the moon. Here was a room lined with gurneys, gurneys covered in sheets, sheets that bore shapes of bodies. Each sheet featured a different Rorschach test of blood. Across from Bridget was a second door, closed. There was a window along one wall that had been covered in a white sheet. Her eyes were adjusting to the light now, but it wasn't entirely clear where all this light was coming from. She saw no lamp, no light bulb. Just surfaces of glowing whiteness blighted only by blood.

She walked between the gurneys.

She smelled something foul. It was an itchy smell that tugged at her sinuses, found purchase somewhere in the back of her throat.

She reached out to touch a sheet, a sheet with a Soviet map of blood over the Urals of a body. She stopped, let her hand hover an inch over it. She imagined that the presence of a real body below would radiate something she could sense, a kind of body heat of the dead, and the fact that she felt nothing told her she could relax.

The door, the second door, opened. Bridget was so startled her body spasmed. Her hand briefly grazed the sheet, felt the forgiving solidity of a body beneath. She stabilized both her hands on her belly and watched a figure walk into the room.

This figure was dressed in a white coat buttoned all the way up. Their face was covered in a white mask the texture of cheesecloth. A white cap covered the rest of their head, leaving only their eyes, which were still smudged with orange frosting. This must have been Anya. But those eyes did not acknowledge Bridget.

Anya, firmly in character, walked over to a gurney in the center of the room. Bridget moved back, as if shrinking into the walls, an involuntary reaction to being completely ignored by another human. She couldn't tell if she was audience or interloper. She wanted to be neither.

Anya reached under the gurney and pulled out a metal bucket. She set the bucket on the floor beside her. She pulled from the bucket a knife as long as her forearm, curved like a small scimitar and serrated with teeth as gnarled as a shark's. Holding it in one hand, she pulled up the middle of the sheet with her other hand. This exposed only a plane of pale flesh at the side of an abdomen. Not enough flesh to see any features like a belly button or the curve of a pubis.

Bridget's hip bumped into another gurney. It wobbled and squeaked against her weight. Anya still did not look back at her.

Anya, hidden under white medical linen, touched the flesh of the cadaver with the end of her serrated blade. She pressed slightly and the skin dimpled in. She moved the tip of the blade up, leaving the little white wake of a scrape.

Bridget felt panic well up in her chest and she stepped forward. "Hey." Bridget reached her hand out, saw a smear of blood on her own fingers.

Then Anya pressed the knife in. The body accepted the blade with a pooling of red, which gathered and fell in streams. Anya pushed the blade to the hilt.

"Anya," Bridget said. "That's you, right? It's me. I helped you frost the cookies!"

Anya kept her eyes on her work. She pushed the blade down, as if cutting a cake. Blood was pooling on the gurney and dripping, pouring, onto the floor. The floor, Bridget saw, was covered in white garbage bags, flattened out and quilted together with duct tape. The pool of blood was expanding at Anya's bootied feet, the pool now creeping toward Bridget.

"Listen, I need you to break character for like half a second, okay? I need you to help me get out of here."

Anya's knife was flat against the bottom of the gurney, having sliced forty-five degrees down the side of the stomach of this veiled body. Anya now turned the blade sideways, as if to laterally torque open the wound. The whole thing opened, viscera blooming out. Like time-lapse footage of flora expanding impossibly into glory, these guts escaped with alarming confidence.

Were these the organs Bridget had harvested herself? Had they since been repackaged into this corporeal sack? Something the size of a mouse, pink, squishy and gooey, flopped to the floor. Its possible function in a body was mysterious, but it quivered slightly as it settled near Anya's left foot.

"Anya," Bridget said, "Listen, I helped you with those cookies, and now I need your help. You seen Jake? I think he was with the Tonies."

Anya, moving achingly slow, set the knife down on top of what might have been the cadaver's sternum, and she pushed her latexed hands into the stomach. The cornucopia of organs accepted her hands, absorbed them.

The smell turned. It became sweeter, with an acidic tang like a cluster of raspberries at the bottom of a compost pile.

The care with which Anya kept the viscera from bloodying

the front of her white coat was impressive, and at odds with that little orange smudge of cookie frosting that had made it all this way on Anya's brow. It was from the imperfections that Bridget most wanted to protect the perfectionist, all of Mabel's little blind spots where Bridget tried to hide.

"Please," Bridget said. "You don't have to help me, but please look at me."

Anya's hands withdrew from the body. Her hands gripped something the size of a burrito, but smoothed a dark maroon. Porous and shiny, the liver had blights of yellow, a darker trim along an ominous seam. Anya held it up in the light.

The cadaver's gut lay open, cavernous and vulgar.

"Anya?" Bridget stepped back.

Anya looked, finally, at Bridget. She was going to speak. Bridget felt relief dilating in her chest like ink on paper. Then Anya's gaze shifted to something behind Bridget.

Bridget turned and saw three people entering the scene: A girl in a skeleton outfit, a guy dressed as a *Clockwork* droog, and Ethan following them holding the Panasonic DV Pro. He was training the video camera on his two peers, catching their visible, if not performative, shock at entering the mock morgue. Ethan was too fixated on their images in the flip-out monitor to notice Bridget.

She backed up, expecting to bump into Anya, but the girl was no longer there; instead, Bridget felt a gurney behind her, felt the soft hush of the fabric on the pads of her fingers.

As the skeleton and the droog wandered among the gurneys, the droog poking at the bodies indiscriminately, Ethan's lens followed. In a moment Bridget would be in view.

She squatted down, scrambled backward on crab legs. Shuffling away, her head hit the edge of another gurney. She tucked beside it, rubbing her temple, and, from underneath the sheet, a hand flopped down. Its limp fingers brushed her cheek. She revolted, slapped the hand away. This only caused the hand to fall further from the gurney, the arm now exposed all the way to the bicep. Bridget had to duck away from it.

The hand curled up, fingers gathering slowly. The arm lifted.

She scooted away to hide beside another gurney. She heard nothing but her own breath. Looking beneath the gurneys for the shoes of Ethan and his friends, she saw only draped sheets. And certainly no sign of Anya's cotton-covered shoes.

From this angle, she could see the body on the gurney whose cover she'd just left. That hand reached up and gathered fingers around the edge of the blood-stained white sheet and began to pull, the sheet sliding slowly down. It revealed first hair, then a forehead, then eyes, closed. This face looked familiar, but in its unanimated form Bridget couldn't confidently identify it. It wasn't until he opened his eyes and began to sit up—stiffly and unnaturally, without the aid of elbows to prop himself up, just the freakish core strength of the young and the dead—that she recognized him as Skylar. His ponytail sat on his shoulder like a ferret. He was not wearing a shirt, the bloodied garment gathered at his waist.

Skylar's eyes were white, cataracted, the object of their gaze impossible to discern. She must have moved without realizing it, because the gurney she was crouched beside rattled. Skylar jolted in her direction. She tried to scurry away but got caught in the sheet he was flinging free.

With the sheet suddenly draped over her, she felt the still-damp blood stain, smelled the ripeness of it. She groped at the sheet, but couldn't pull it off, couldn't find the edges. She got to her feet, kept pulling at the sheet. It seemed to encompass her whole body. She stepped forward, hands out, caught as if in a net.

She was exposed now, no use pretending to hide—a woman fighting to free herself from a sheet. She called out "Hello? Guys?"

Then the lights, which had glared through the sheet, went out.

A hand gripped her bicep. She tried to twist away, but Anya's voice—her mouth close enough to trouble the fabric at Bridget's ears—said, "This way, quick."

She let the teenager guide her. Across the room, the cackles and curses of Ethan and his friends functioned as sonar and told her Anya was leading her away from them.

The girl's hand soon placed Bridget's hand on a doorknob, then pulled the cadaver sheet from her head. Anya said, "Don't be stupid—go."

In the moment it took Bridget to get oriented in the still-dark room, Anya was gone.

"Thanks," Bridget whispered.

She turned the doorknob. She pushed the door open, saw nothing. She walked toward that nothing, closing the door behind her.

Her hands discovered the topography of what seemed to be an empty closet. She found no hanging clothes, no bar above. There was, however, against the back wall, another door. It was small, about half the size of a normal door, and it opened up at her torso. She reached inside and felt nothing but a breeze moving the otherwise stale air. Behind her, on the other side of the door through which she'd entered this enclosure, she heard screams—screams that began with the squeal of people enjoying the thrills, screams that quickly frayed into something genuine. She lifted her right leg, positioned her knee into the space this new tiny door offered, and she pulled herself into it.

Once her belly was in—her center of gravity, of self—she could easily pull the rest of her body in, tucking her legs up and closing the door behind her. Closing this door took some careful work, pincering the very edge of the little door with her fingertips, as there was no interior doorknob or even latch. Folded into this new space, she finally realized what it was: a dumbwaiter.

This little box of a place, though, perfectly fit her body, as long as that body had its limbs folded neatly around her belly. It was oddly comforting, containing. She breathed in the scent of her forearms, crossed over her chest. She smelled, too, the gossamer plastic of her purple wig, remembered it was still on her head. She could just stay here and everything would work out just fine—maybe even better—without her. In the distant future, when the anthropologists of the post-Anthropocene would be dusting through the last vestiges of Clinton-era decadence, they'd find a woman's skeleton inside a wooden box inside a house. Unconcerned with the questions that were currently choking her brain like vines—questions about what had happened that night on the phone, between Jake and his dad—they would find of her the only thing that would be left: the dense rubber of her belly topped with a bad wig, the only nonbiodegradables to survive whatever disaster lay in wait, her pregnancy preserved for posterity, all that potential still in gestation.

Her hands brushed something scratchy and hempy: a rope in the corner of her box. She grabbed hold of it. She pulled down with minimal weight and felt resistance, but a resistance that spoke of something metallic and operable above, a pulley.

Both hands on the rope, she began hefting herself up in her little wooden box, about a foot at a time. When she needed a break, she paused, one hand on the rope, and her free hand grazed an impression in the wood that seemed to suggest she was already at another door. Her hand felt for the seam, the crack, and sure enough she could now hear the terror of their music with greater clarity.

She pushed the little door open and, instead of being greeted by her son, she saw a scene of blood splatter in black light. The little dumbwaiter door offered a window into a room where a man in a leather apron and hockey mask was wielding a chainsaw against a ribbony tangle of meat hanging from the ceiling. Around him, human corpses, in various stages of undress, hung from meat hooks, hands tied at their waists, mouths gagged. Their eyes open, one of them spotted Bridget and started writhing on his hook and screaming against his gag.

Bridget gripped both hands on the rope and furiously ascended the dumbwaiter shaft, leaving the huff of chainsaw below her. When she'd pulled her little box far enough to find a new door, the screams from the butcher's room were distant and her arms were going rubbery with strain.

She shoved her body to the side and she fell into a darkened space, defined only by the hardness of its floor. On that floor, her body having instinctively angled itself to protect her belly from the impact, she heard the dumbwaiter, its weight no longer managed by her grip, fall all the way back down.

She saw only the Terminator eye of a dim red light, and before her eyes could adjust, she got to her feet and moved toward it.

● **REC**

Every attempt to look only points to what is unseen. The frame is always too tight on the effects—zooming in on broken glass on the ground, a boot smearing something into carpet—that the causes, the people, are omitted. You know their presence only by the occasional violence they do to the frame. It shakes, is always rattled by someone unseen.

16.

A simple hallway emerged before her in shades of blue. Two doorways were up ahead, but here, within arm's reach, the little red light turned out to be from a wall-mounted phone. Instead of making her way down the hallway immediately, she decided to linger here at the phone, a little lighthouse in the night. She picked it up just for the glow of its rubbery number pad.

What exactly had Jake said to his dad? Had it been Tod's idea for Jake to come home or Jake's? Jake didn't have it in him to do that. It must have been Tod who'd offered, who'd said come home. She hadn't spoken to Tod in—how long? She couldn't remember. Units of time played three-card Monte in her head. Maybe all Jake had to do was dial. A year on the road had surely taught Jake that the trick was making the other guy think it was his idea, and that meant timing, knowing the exact right moment to dial that number. Those familiar digits blooped beneath her fingertips with the ease of playing a familiar tune. She was just trying the number out, though. She would stop at the final digit, then hang up. She would. Except she didn't.

It was now ringing, a soft note quavering in the quiet hallway, the receiver a hand's length from her ear.

She needed a plan, now. If he picked up—and of course he would: Tod wasn't the kind to be out at this time of night, unless he'd become the type to be out at this time of night—she would just be calling to confirm Jake's story, that's all. *Just calling to make sure that Jake's story about returning home checked out—because you know Jake and his slippery way with the truth—and how was everything with you? Great, great, okay, well I should let you go now, take care.* It was a simple plan, formulated in the seconds between rings, seconds dilated by terror, but it would do.

Unless—

Another ring.

—she could ask for help. Stupidly simple, no angle, but she could. Tell Tod that she and Jake were stuck here, that they were in trouble. And how far were they from Denver? She'd lost track.

The next ring was interrupted by a click, the blessed click of the answering machine activating. She felt the constriction in her chest loosen, and she pulled the receiver from her face to hang up, but then she heard not the outgoing greeting of Tod droning, "I'm sorry we cannot come to the phone at the moment," but rather a sharp and raspy "Yes?"

Bridget held the receiver in front of her face, its number pad illuminated in the darkened hallway like Mabel's old Lite-Brite, the voice emerging from it: Mabel's.

That hoarseness was something new, an affectation or illness, Bridget could not be sure, but she needed to hear more, needed to swaddle herself in her daughter's voice.

Mabel, as if obliging, said, "Hello?" unpacking two syllables into three.

She could ask Mabel for help. Or not help, just tell her to drive out here and get them, no questions.

Bridget started to say "Hello," but, feeling the tremor in her voice, she switched, mid-word, to the single chirp of "Hi." The result, as the phone receiver fed her own aspirated voice back into her ear, was not quite either word, while still tonally recognizable as a greeting.

Behind her, in the dumbwaiter shaft, there was a rattling.

"Who is this?" Mabel said, her voice clearing.

Bridget felt the blood draining from her head, the world quickly retreating. "It's me." She coiled the phone cord, as long as a jump rope, around her index finger.

"What are you selling?"

This stopped Bridget like a jab to the solar plexus. Did the sound of Bridget's voice immediately put Mabel on the defensive, ready to parry off some scheme? So much for Jake's claim that Tod was no longer angry; he'd clearly been tutoring Mabel on Bridget's history of deceit, preparing her to treat Bridget's reemergence as that of a mere huckster. Bridget wished, in that moment, that she really was just a dial-a-scam drone.

Unless—

"Do you even exist or are you a robocaller?"

—Mabel really didn't recognize her, genuinely thought this was an unsolicited sales call.

Her voice like tissue paper, Bridget said, "I exist." But the exact nature of her existence seemed, for once, to be up to her. The devastation of Mabel not recognizing her voice was lined with gratitude: her daughter was inadvertently offering her a way out.

"Prove it," Mabel said.

The rattling behind her continued, got louder.

"I'm just calling to," Bridget said—accommodate—"ask if you'd like an opportunity for an all-expense paid trip to the lap of luxury? Of course you would." She corrected her posture, corrected it from the italicized lean of Bridget to the rigidity of someone else, someone who didn't matter. "Here at Vespucci Travel, we're offering—" And what was Bridget offering? To herself, an opportunity to face rejection in the character of a salesperson, rather than as herself. To Mabel, permission to hang up. "We're offering a once-in-a-lifetime opportunity—for escape."

"Sounds rad," Mabel said.

Bridget crushed the phone against her ear.

Mabel continued: "You know what else sounds rad, person who definitely exists?"

"What?" The rattling from the dumbwaiter was metallic, insistent.

"Me star sixty-nining you and calling you back in the middle of the night and waking your ass up. You're gonna wish you were a robocaller then, huh."

Bridget balled curlicues of cord in her fist. "I'm sorry."

Mabel exhaled rage into the receiver, distorted the signal. "I was waiting for a *real* call from a *real* person, and now he's probably getting a busy signal."

A gentleman caller, Bridget thought, as if watching herself, and not without some comfort, metamorphose into some Edwardian pearl-clutcher. Maybe this was the character of the Vespucci sales rep emerging.

"All because," Mable was saying, "of a telemarketer in some call center out in Asshole, Arizona."

Scenes of this alluded-to social life—of the phone cord snaking beneath the door of her teenage daughter's room, of snapping rejection that signaled not anger but lunges away from childhood and the infantilizing concern of a parent—came into immediate focus, and Bridget ached for those stiff-armed rebukes, ached to see Mabel's own metamorphosis.

"We have call waiting," Bridget said.

"I'm hanging up now."

In the moment before the click, Bridget nodded and said, "Love you." It just snuck out, a thing escaped, feral.

She slammed the receiver back on the wall mount, crushed it as if to gag the thing quiet.

The rattling behind her continued.

Had Mabel caught that escaped utterance? The possibility had her by the throat.

Then the phone rang. It was a noise loud enough to blot out thought, consciousness. The jaggedness of the ring seemed manifest in her hands, now shaking.

The rattling behind her continued, undeterred.

The phone rang again, the sound serrated. She extended her hand, unsteady.

The ring, the rattle, in a moment the two geared together into a sound that animated her body into a mad dash down the hall. That sound, it chased her. It chased her through the door at the end of the hall, which revealed itself to be a cluttered broom closet. Then the sound chased her through the door opposite, which led down a small flight of stairs, then into a narrow, low-ceilinged hallway, which wended around multiple turns, its wooden walls shedding glossy peels of paint beneath her fingers. Taking those blind corners with increasing speed, she kept one hand out, one hand on her belly.

Back when her babies were growing into the age when referring to them aloud as babies elicited groaning teenage ire, she would still imagine the vanishing twin syndrome that her stylist had foretold. When both Mabel and Jake were in the same room, side by side, what was once parallel play becoming mutually divergent, she began to understand that implicit in those scenarios of vanishing twin syndrome was a choice: she, or some part of her that she wasn't on speaking terms with, always had to decide who to imagine as the surviving twin.

The anxiety that crept into her relationship with Mable always felt like a stifled urge to apologize.

In the dark of this hallway, Bridget almost ran face-first into Caleb.

She said, "Oh."

"Hi, there," he said, blocking her way. His face was ghoulish from the flashlight he held.

"Caleb!" She clapped her hands together, once. "Are you ready? Do you want to run your lines before we put it to tape? Where can we do this? Somewhere quiet, I hope? Other than that, we just need a white wall and a good light. And you, of course. It's all about you, buddy!" The old scripts stuck in her mind not necessarily because they worked but because they were the old scripts. "Have you seen Ethan? I saw him running around with my camera. I'll need that, of course." She felt the old confidence reinflating her chest. "Let's get moving, honey."

She shooed him back. But he didn't move. She held out her hand, in both greeting and defense.

He reached out, too, slowly, toward her face. His fingers pinched a few strands of her purple wig. He pulled the wig from her head, held it up with dispassionate curiosity. She tried to reach for the wig, but he dropped it and grabbed her wrist. "What *is* your name?"

Her foot shot out, another reflex. It made contact with his knee, and his legs buckled. As he fell—oddly forward, his legs giving out beneath him—he collided with her, and what might have otherwise been a small stumble now pinballed their two bodies against the walls, then to the floor.

She landed on her back. He landed on top of her. The flashlight rolled beside her head. As he pushed himself up, he pushed one of her boobs, too clumsily to be intentional. He stood up, grabbed the flashlight, and froze, shone the light on her belly, his face struck in shock.

"When did that happen?" Caleb pointed to her belly. "I—I didn't notice." Then the fall seemed to telescope back into his brain and he snapped to. "Oh! Are you okay?" He crouched down, addressing her belly, hands hovering out, as if to help but not wanting to actually touch her stomach. "I didn't hurt it, did I?"

She put her hands on her belly, though it was the rest of her that hurt.

"Okay," he was saying, trying to pull her gently to her feet. "I'm sorry, ma'am."

On her feet, she kept her hands on her belly, her face down.

Caleb said, "I promise I didn't realize you were—like that."

With each breath, she gave a moan.

"Does it hurt?" He guided her through a dimly lit hall. "Here, I know a good place to lay you down."

He led her through a room spastic with lights like the inside of a concussion, walls densely cobwebbed, skeleton arms reaching out from the walls, fingering their faces as they passed through. He led her through a hallway puddled with what appeared to be blood. He led her through a room dense with a malarial fog. The floor felt squishy like a bog, something swimming between their feet. And he led her into a room with a warm hearth-like glow to it, a nice change of pace.

In the moment it took her eyes to focus, she asked, "Where are we?"

In the center of the room, a bed of hay sat invitingly. He helped her down onto the hay. It was warm. There were figures, still blurry, surrounding her.

"The zombie manger," Caleb said.

The figures were in hoods, and beneath the hoods faces scored with scratches and runny with pus. Coming into focus, the undead magi, she saw, were done-up mannequins.

Caleb crouched next to her. "You feel any pain? We took quite the tumble. I'm so sorry. They didn't tell me you were like that. I didn't notice, I guess. You feel any pain?"

She said, "I do."

"Just stay like that, then." Caleb stood up. "I'll go get some help."

And, before she could come up with something to stop him, he was gone.

As the three decomposing wise men watched her with plastic eyes, Bridget tried to enjoy a moment of repose and imagined that the severed heads these ghoulish well-wishers were holding were gifts she actually needed. Not that a severed head was any less useful to her than some frankincense was to Joseph and Mary. Frankincense was what, some kind of perfume? When she was recovering from giving birth to the twins, Tod's mother brought her large Ziploc bags full of her partially used makeup. The plastic of the bag was opaque with flesh-tone residue. Tod's mother had thought that all Bridget needed was to freshen up, to look good in order to feel good. And to help mitigate Bridget's rage at that bag of makeup, Tod applied some of it on himself, offering her a grotesquery of himself (he'd been weirdly skittish about getting the lipstick directly on his lips, so he ringed it just outside of his lips for a truly clownish grin).

It occurred to her that enjoying a moment of repose was exactly the wrong thing to do just now. She started to prop herself back up.

The door to the zombie manger opened. Bertram Cline walked in.

Bridget scrambled, tried to get to her feet, but Bertram was already standing above her. He crouched down and placed his hand on her shoulder. The gesture appeared comforting, but he exerted real pressure on her shoulder, holding her down.

"Sorry for the getup," he said, gesturing to the white doctor's coat he was wearing, splattered with blood. "I had to fill in for someone."

Bridget tried to make eye contact with the wise men. They gazed emptily at the space behind her. She silently implored the inanimate for help; that seemed easier than it had been to ask her daughter.

"How do you like the show?" Bertram asked.

Bridget grasped at the hay beneath her. "Nice." She knew to stick to single syllables; anything more complex would reveal the tremor in her voice.

"Just nice?" He tightened his lips in disappointment, his eyes drifting around the manger. He fiddled with something just behind Bridget. "You can give me more honest feedback than that. I'm not fragile. I can take it. Come on, you're in show business. I want to know what you really think."

His halitosis was frosted with mint mouthwash. The door behind him was closed. In a house filled with ersatz terror, what good was one more scream? She said, "Why?"

Bertram's smile seemed dimmed beneath other, more pressing concerns. "I'm a producer on this whole thing. It's not just glue sticks and Hefty bags anymore. These things require real monetary investment—if you're going to do it right."

Bridget now felt like she could muster more than a monosyllable. More than capable, she felt compelled. "It's all very—effective."

Bertram nodded. He had been squatting before her for long enough that he now needed to adjust his legs. When he did so, he put an arm on her thigh and, as he shifted his weight, he pushed down on her, hard. Something metal in his white coat grazed her knee. "That's good to know," he said. "I like to be diligent in all things. I'm not just a guy who writes checks—though, of course, you know that I do write checks." His smile seemed more genuine now, more immediate, his teeth parted as if to bite an amuse-bouche. "I'm an active investor—in the community. After all, I'm the guy on the school board who got the good doctor's hire approved. Not a small feat after what happened before. Point is, I have high expectations and I'm exacting. I used to say I'm a perfectionist, but it was Ethan—my son, you know him—who pointed out that my perfectionism is just competitiveness. He was right. I like being better than others, and I'm good at it. But you can only achieve that by being humble and valuing honest feedback. So, little miss—what's your name again?"

Bridget's mouth was dry, but she said her name, her real one.

Mouth closed, lips relaxed, Bertram seemed to chew on this. Then he said, "So. Your honest feedback. How do you like the show? Really."

"You're very good at this."

"At what?"

"The show of it all, the spectacle of—"

"Death?"

"I guess so, yeah."

"I'm not, though."

"You're not?"

He shook his head. "I'm good at getting people to do what I tell them to do. Our good doctor out there, he's good at making pain look—compelling." He removed from his coat pocket a scalpel. "I'm sloppy at that sort of thing."

Bridget said, "I just want to go home."

Bertram pursed his lips. "Too late." His nostrils whistled. "You took something from me."

"I can get it. Just let me get my son and I'll return it all."

He shook his head. "Do I look like someone whose bank was broken by your little stunt?"

"I don't understand. You don't want the money back?"

"I'm saying that's not what I want."

She said, "Okay?" She offered a smile. The gesture he returned involved him tightening his mouth in an upward curve, but it could not be described as a smile.

"What you took is not what you owe," he said. "It never is."

She tried to sit up, but he placed his hand back on her shoulder.

"When you pay a debt," he said, "you're not returning money. You're returning time, something ineffable. I could have given you that money and not thought twice. But what you took was something different. Without the confidence that I can protect them from intruders, then my family is not a family. It's just a collection of idiots living in the same house." He held the scalpel casually, seemingly unaware of it. "Someone like you doesn't know that."

"I have a family," she said.

He cocked his head. "No, you don't."

He stuck the scalpel in.

● **REC**

A closeup of a woman's face. It's clear, from the jitteriness of the frame, the soft edges of her face, that you are watching from a considerable distance. She fills the frame in a way both intimate and alienating, the zoom that carries you across this distance emphasizing that remove as much as it bridges it. The woman's face, in three-quarters profile, looks down, eyes following the line of her nose, fixed on something unseen.

17.

Bridget felt nothing. The scalpel was lodged in her abdomen, and she felt nothing.

Bertram Cline looked down. Bridget looked down. They both saw the scalpel sticking bloodlessly from her belly.

Bertram looked at Bridget. His eyes twitched in confusion, then fear.

She put her hands behind her, pushed herself up. He moved back, gave her room. As she got to her feet, he remained crouched. Their faces passed each other in chiasmus. When his face was beneath hers, she noticed the wise men behind him, all staring dumbly at the blade stuck in her pregnant belly. The blade was now eye-level with Bertram.

Struck silent by the sight, he fell back. He didn't seem to notice his own body tumbling back onto the floor, so absorbed was he in the specter of this woman whose pregnant body could absorb his violence with such aplomb.

She, too, was taken with the sight of it: the handle of the blade emerging like a sundial from the planula of her belly.

She stepped past Bertram. She stepped past the zombie magi. She opened the door and was gone.

In the hall, black lights turned all sights inside out.

She walked through a labyrinth of halls, looking for the

stairs. She walked over puddles of blood starting to scab over, crunchy like ice beneath her feet.

No, you don't, the man had said. While Jake was awaiting a judge to officially declare him emancipated, from family, from her, she had now received another ruling, equally definitive. But Jake, if she found him, if she took him back, from this, from everything, he was hers.

All hallways led to the stairs. But she soon found, at the top of the stairs, on a low-ceilinged landing, Dr. Docter. He was standing on a stool, securing what appeared to be shrunken heads to a chandelier.

She paused, obscured—she hoped—in the darkness of the hallway. It occurred to her that she might be able to simply sneak past him. His body was angled away from where the hallway met the stairs, with just enough room behind his stool for her to slink by. He was clearly occupied in his task, and the air was still clotted with the music of the dead—maybe he just wouldn't notice her scooting by. That was unrealistic, and she felt embarrassed for even entertaining the thought. There was no getting by him undetected. Jake's theory of shoplifting, refined in the hours they'd accumulated in shopping malls, was that it wasn't the stealing that got you caught but the fear; people only attracted the attention of the loss prevention guys when they were too nervous to just walk out the door. Or so he'd observed. When he'd floated this theory, she made sure he knew that they didn't do that sort of thing, that they were a different class of people. Yes, yes, he knew—he was just saying, was all. So, she'd said, getting away with it was just a trick of self-possession. Well, he'd responded, now she was sounding like Zig Ziglar. But if you had to sneak out, you were doing it wrong.

She stepped out of the shadows and toward the stairs. She put greater distance between each step.

"Excuse me," she said as she stepped through the narrow space between his stool and the corner where the hallway met the landing.

"You been getting a lot of mileage out of that costume," Dr. Docter said. He was looking down at her as if checking to see what he'd stepped in. His left hand held the descending arm of the chandelier, while his right hand gripped a raisin-shriveled head.

Bridget took a breath. "It suits me." She had one foot on the landing, the other on the first step down. Beneath them, downstairs, songs from different rooms were competing, slipping from harmony to discord and back again.

"I'll need it back," Dr. Docter said.

Bridget touched her belly. "Of course. These things aren't meant to be permanent." Her hand grazed the scalpel still sticking out. "It's a wonderful show you put on. Every year?"

"The haunted house usually isn't this haunted." He returned to securing the shrunken head. Focused on the task, his eyes were impossible to read.

From down the hall, which disappeared into darkness, came the slow shuffle of movement.

"People keep stealing these," he said. "And I keep putting new ones up. The things they make you do, huh?"

Eyes trying to focus on the unseen end of the hallway, Bridget said, "Who?"

"Kids," he said. He sighed, assessed his work, this mobile of the macabre. "This whole thing is just—out of control."

Bridget went down another step, moving out of view of the dark maw of that hallway. "Kinda late to realize that."

"I've always known it. That's the deal. That's what we sign up for."

"We? Did I sign up for this?" Her hand touched the banister.

"But," he said, "being a parent isn't pushing the chaos away. It's curating the chaos, to give the illusion of control." He was still barefoot, his callus-less feet on the corrugated rubber of the footstool. "That's what we do, right?"

"We?"

"That boy—yours, right?"

"My associate?"

He looked down at her, smiled. "Still in character, huh?"

"I'm just on my way out. We both are. We're all done here. Promise." She wrapped her hand around the scalpel's handle, cold, crosshatched for grip. "We're going."

"My buddy Bertram is looking for you. Hand me the next one, huh?" He nodded at the grocery bag beside the footstool, filled with shrunken heads, eyes stitched shut.

She took her hand off the scalpel, reached down, grabbed one of the heads, felt its leathery scalp. She squeezed it like a stress ball, found its squishy resistance satisfying. She handed it up to him. He accepted it with his right hand. With his left hand, he gripped one of the chandelier's arms, festooned with little metal hooks. His tungsten carbide wedding band caught the light from below. With his right hand, he began affixing the head to one of those decorative hooks.

"Where'd you say you're headed?"

"Home."

For some reason, she thought of Ms. Rombauer, that awful teacher who'd threatened Jake with tests. Jake was wrong about her. He didn't know anything. Bridget had protected him.

Dr. Docter said, "No, you're not."

She kicked the footstool out from under his legs.

His body fell—not to the floor, but like a body through a gallows. He went snap, pulled tight. The shrunken head fell to the floor, bounced. Dr. Docter was balancing on the very tip of his right foot. His left hand remained above his head, his black wedding band having caught a hook on the arm of the chandelier. His face was a rictus of pain inexpressible. He wasn't screaming. He didn't appear to be breathing. His body was a straight line from his left ring finger to his right foot. His big toe bore all his weight. Unnaturally extended from his hand, his ring finger was quickly turning from red to purple. His eyes were on her. They, too, seemed extended unnaturally from his skull.

"Just breathe," she said. She backed down the stairs. "Your body takes care of the rest."

His big toe on pointe, his finger was now noticeably longer. She heard the slight creak of tendon, the medical professional's phalanges getting pulled from his hand. He was holding his breath as if it was the only thing he had.

She turned and rushed down the stairs, two, three steps at a time.

By the time she reached the bottom, she heard his slow-motion scream, the potato-sack sound of his body collapsing to the floor. That indestructible ring must have done its work, the terrible work of extraction, pulled the finger the rest of the way out, slow enough to feel every pop, every tear.

She'd find Jake, take him back.

When she turned down a hallway with bleeding walls, she ran into a figure who screamed before he came into focus. The guy had his yellow stun gun drawn, extended, and in the moment it took her to figure out who this was who was suddenly smashed against her body—the adolescent-looking security guard for the neighborhood—she also realized that he was sending an impotent shock into her belly. The realization seemed to hit him in the same moment, as his face—pulling back from a blurred Picasso-mess into an actual face—registered a kind of horror that veered toward awe.

"Sorry, sorry, sorry," he was now saying. He pulled his stun gun back, held it at a distance with one hand. With his other hand, he guided her down to sit on the floor, her back against the gummy blood. Crouching over her, addressing her belly, he said, "Did I do that one, too?" He pointed his stun gun at the scalpel.

She grabbed the stun gun from his hand. He seemed relieved to let her have it.

He said, "Maybe it'll be okay? The fella in there? Maybe they can just absorb things like this," pointing to the stun gun, "and that," pointing to the scalpel. "It's not even full voltage. They won't let me until I pass the exam."

"Just go," she said.

"Right. I'll go ask someone for help." He looked around the hallway, lights strobing red. "Thing is, they don't know I'm real. They threw things at me when I came in, so I told them this was just a costume, like you said, and then they let me stay. But I'll go get someone to help."

"No," she said. "Just go."

She pointed the stun gun at his chest, its plastic bulk like a toy.

"Right away, ma'am." He stood up. "You invited me, you know." And then he was gone.

Bridget pushed herself up.

Down the hallway, she followed the sound: no longer just music but the dense clutter of bodies.

Armed, she could see herself out, once she had her son. Once she had Jake, she would leave, they would leave.

When she walked into the living room, the scalpel still emerging like the jackstaff of the great ship that was her belly, and she found herself in the midst of a dance party. The performance of the haunted house had been eroded by drunkenness and exhaustion, and now both attendees and attendants were writhing together to the belching beats of something like music.

And here was Jake. Sitting on a loveseat, squished between the Tonies, staring up at the wall that was showing *Halloween*, possibly on a loop, the soundtrack inaudible in the din. He was just sitting there, with a couple of other kids, watching a movie.

She'd get him home. Of course. And of course Jake would be welcomed back and resume his life as if none of this had happened, a derailment for her merely a detour for him. He'd pick up where he'd left off. He'd enroll in community college, take those engineering and film courses he'd found in the catalog when it'd arrived in dim newsprint years ago. He would live at home for a while, and he would—

On the other side of the living room, a little red recording light on her Panasonic DV Pro glared at her, the same light she'd once covered with black electrical tape so as to not spook timid Ethan—Ethan who was now training that lens directly at her.

—rebuild something with Tod. Jake would bring home movies he'd learned about in his Intro the Film class and watch them with his father, movies about Experiences that were themselves Experiences, movies made by and for people who'd never aided and abetted their mothers' felonies, and part of his return to life would be to feign naivete until it felt natural again, to become a passive audience member again, and to turn to Tod, to his dad, and say things like, "That shootout was sick," and—

Behind Ethan, people were gathering, figures too dark to identify—perhaps Bertram, perhaps the nine-fingered doctor, perhaps the security guard, perhaps Caleb—figures whose attention Ethan was now pointing to her, those figures in the opposite direction of the path that was clear, the path between her and the foyer and the open front door.

—Tod would say, "Yeah," because Tod would be part of the fiction, too, the fiction required to assimilate his son back into something like this life. And Jake would see Mabel head off to a four-year college, and maybe he'd realize that wasn't for him, but he'd find his own niche soon enough, maybe in L.A., where he'd find work on a set, become like all those guys she'd seen in her youth, guys who knew where things went, how things worked, and those were the things that would provide him with the structure for a life. And maybe she wouldn't be there for that, but she could get him there.

Standing behind the loveseat, she squeezed his shoulder. "It's time to go home, Jake."

He did not turn around, just waved his hand at her.

One of the Tonies, looking back at her, said, "Ryan, you got a zombie coming for you."

It started then as a flicker in her peripheral vision, like an eye floater or a neurological glitch: a little pucker in the air. Then it landed on the top of her son's head. It was a butterfly. Not a monarch, nothing so easily identifiable and reproducible on an iron-on patch, this butterfly was the color of—though maybe this was a trick of the red-gel lights of the party—a watercolor palette gone aswirl with unmanaged paints.

Bridget said, "We have to leave."

Jake, eyes on the screen above, said, "I want to see how this ends."

Jake didn't notice the creature perched on his head. She imagined holding it gently in her palm, feeling its wings like eyelashes on her skin, and then she'd place it in her mouth, and she imagined it would feel like a nasturtium on her tongue, delicate and pliant and unsuspecting and forgiving against her bite.

Bridget said, "We have to leave."

She remembered Jake as a little kid, the way he'd get in the grocery store, becoming so transfixed by the sights—the phantasmagoric candy displays, the uncanny spectacle of the lobsters in the tank—that he would refuse to leave. She'd always threaten to leave him behind, and he'd always say, "Okay."

Bridget said, "We have to leave."

Jake said nothing.

A second butterfly landed on the back of Jake's hand. He held his hand up for inspection, as if curious how he'd inadvertently become so hospitable to such a delicate thing, its wings so thin, so tearable, now moving back and forth, idly flexing at the pace of a calm breath. And she felt something on the side of her own neck, the light touch of tarsus.

Bridget said, "I have to leave."

Jake said, "Okay."

And even after she made it out the front door through a proliferation of butterflies, and made it out to the car, and even after she tore off the belly and let it flop there in the street so she could fit behind the wheel of the Camry without messing with the stubborn seat, and even after she made it back to the motel and started packing up with the stun gun placed on the nightstand just in case, and even after someone knocked on the door and she had to take up the stun gun to ask who it was, plastic weapon poised beside the chain-lock as she heard Jake's voice, and even after he came in and explained that the Tonies had dropped him off, it was in the tiny, darkened room of that "Okay" that she lived.

For all the driving they'd done that year, though, they weren't too far from home.

She said, "I'll drop you off a block early, then?"

He said, "Okay."

Acknowledgments

I could not have completed this novel without the help and good humor of Diana Thow. For his diligence and insight, I'm grateful to Kevin Breen. Finally, I deeply appreciate the support of the New Literary Project.

About the Author

Kevin Allardice is the author of four novels, including *Any Resemblance to Actual Persons*, which was long-listed for the Center for Fiction's First Novel Prize. His most recent book is *The Ghosts of Bohemian Grove*. In 2022, Allardice was a Jack Hazard Fellow with the New Literary Project. He and his family live in the Bay Area.

CPSIA information can be obtained
at www.ICGtesting.com
Printed in the USA
JSHW032043090423
40106JS00006B/23

9 781960 59300